THE ORCHARD HOUSE

Ruth Tomalin

A DAY IN THE COUNTRY IV

Everything is only for a day: that which remembers and that which is remembered.

Marcus Aurelius

THE ORCHARD HOUSE

Published in 2008 by YouWriteOn.com

Published by YouWriteOn.com

I.

The poor, the outcast, knave, child, stranger, fool
Need no commending to the merciful....

Walter de la Mare: A Prayer

1.

Three knocks.

"Silence! Be upstanding in court!" called an usher. "All manner of persons having anything to do before the Queen's justices, draw nigh and give your attendance. God save the Queen and this horrible Bench."

A part-heard case was resumed. A young draughtsman had been charged with forgery and with failing 'on divers occasions' to pay his train fare. He was said to have tried to recoup a month's losses, after a rail strike, by altering the date on his season ticket.

The line of prosecution witnesses showed no signs of ending. The jury, all ears on the first afternoon, now looked resigned. They settled down to a long morning of technical evidence, questions and counter-questions about the marks on the ticket.

In the court next door another case went more briskly on its way. The chief witness, a little spry lady in a black velvet toque, was beckoned into the box. In shy and dignified tones she began her evidence, waiting quietly whenever she was interrupted by shouts from the two burly young women in the dock.

These two were accused of unlawful entry, assault, theft, uttering threats, demanding money with menaces. A welfare officer had promised to find a suitable lodger to keep the old lady company while her husband - a sea captain, still active in his seventies - was away from home. The marauding pair had got into her flat by claiming to be 'from the welfare,' they held her prisoner for a week while they ran riot, cashing her pension cheque, selling her valuables to buy drink, ransacking the place in search of hidden savings which she, despite blows, threats, sleepless nights and near starvation, refused to hand over. One night, while they snored after a drunken brawl, she had escaped by climbing out of a window and crawling along a narrow ledge, sixty feet from the ground, to a neighbour's balcony.

In a third court, what had seemed a simple 'wilful damage to property' was turning into something more complicated. The parties were Indian. Relatives, simmering, crowded the public gallery. The defiant-looking youth on trial had been arrested when he went to a house after dark and hurled a brick through a window. His counsel said he admitted this; but there was great provocation. Inside the house was a girl whom he had married some time before, naturally assuming that she would go to live with him. But her family had since refused to let him see or speak to her, saying that she was a Christian and would not accept the marriage without the blessing of her own Church.

There followed an account of ceremonies already completed: two days' ritual at the bride's home; on the third day, the bridegroom's procession to her house, and a further evening of celebration, the bride still veiled, before they again separated for the fourth and fifth day .....

2

The chairman had so far seemed to drowse, his head bent, showing only the top of an ancient grimy wig. Now he looked up, sighed, pushed back the wig and asked the question bemusing many other listeners in court ..... "And when *are* they allowed to get together?"

Meanwhile the first court had come near to catastrophe. Halfway through the morning, a woman on the jury insisted on having a note passed to the clerk, saying that she felt she must ask a question. Given permission, she stood up, quaking visibly, to explain that something had been worrying her since the case had begun. Should she really be on this jury? She herself was employed by British Rail.

A great groan went up. The chairman put his head in his hands. The prosecution case was nearly completed. Hours of intricate testimony had passed. Must all this go for nothing? A new jury, a fresh start?

But chairman, clerk and counsel, conferring, decided that the case might continue with eleven jurors. "Madam," she was told bitterly, "you may go." Poor Madam, cutting short her apologies, scuttled out of court; Judge Huff sending after her a venomous look that said - *And just take her head off outside.*

On the Bench a visiting woman magistrate - fortyish, in grey with touches of white, and matching hat - murmured to the chairman, perhaps showing sympathy with the unhappy juror. Judge Huff twitched crossly, turning the acid-drop tucked into his cheek. Last night he would have asked his clerk with gloom, "And what dolts am I sitting with tomorrow?"

An elderly ticket-collector, who had stopped the accused man and confiscated his ticket, went on giving evidence, glaring at prosecuting counsel as though each question were a calculated insult. In the press seat a young girl with a notebook was joined by another girl. They whispered together and tiptoed out of court.

The woman magistrate looked rather wistfully after them. Long ago, at their age, she too had come into this court, a student taking a 'course in journalism' at the university. This pioneer venture had been devised by an optimistic don, who thought the standards of popular papers might be raised if younger entrants could be caught, fresh from school, and shown how to extend their education.

To the rest of the university - and any working journalists she had met - this seemed a frivolous waste of time. But the course was designed, they were told, to help one find a special subject and get down to some real work. And so, in her case, it had; though not for a newspaper. She'd decided to become secretary to an MP like Sir Evelyn De Courcy, the charmer who had invited them to the Strangers' Gallery. As a first step she joined a student political group, and there she met her husband, bright, ambitious, reading law, and in his way quite as taking as Sir Evelyn. And now, after years as wife, mother and loyal party worker, here she was in 1955,back in the same court, and actually on the Bench. And there were those two young things, trainee reporters evidently, bare-headed, in those casual pretty clothes ... no prim requests from the Bench nowadays that 'lady students' should wear hats, or leave the court while unsuitable cases were heard ... the only creatures in sight who looked carefree, fresh and hopeful; ready for anything in fact, as she and June and Olivia must have looked. One hoped they'd have a little time to enjoy themselves before anything caught up with them.

2.

The courts rose at four. In the press room underground - an ancient cell, far too insalubrious for prisoners nowadays - typewriters clattered, tobacco smoke thickened, vile tea was brewed and drunk. The two juniors, Sarah and Rowan, addressed envelopes to suburban papers and read copy on the telephone to captious Fleet Street copytakers.

Coming out at last into the bright May evening, they dropped into one of the new coffee bars to drink scalding black coffee topped with foam - 'froffy coffee,' still a novelty - and to read the old lady's escape story on the front of the evening papers.

A girl of their own age followed them in; a tall graceful person, pink cheeked and golden haired. She roamed about, singing to herself, choosing cakes from various trolleys, swaying and dancing, her brilliant eyes fixed on some inward vision. A hush fell. The customers looked on with curiosity, the staff huddled behind their counter like hens fascinated by a stoat, willing her to leave before they had to do something about her. It seemed they were in luck. Pocketing several cakes, absently nibbling another, she swayed past the cash desk, in and out of the trellises and rubber plants, out and away.

"High as a kite," said a knowing voice.

Sarah countered - "Or a drama student? A clever hungry one?"

Next morning they were sent together to a 'gang warfare' case. There had been rumours of a rescue plot; the great gates of the court were closed, police swarmed outside, people waiting for admission were scrutinised. No slipping in the back door today; a policeman barred their way, demanding to see their new press passes.

"Oh Tim. You do know us by now."

"Orders, chicks."

Sarah rummaged furiously, then turned her bag upside down, strewing the pavement with notebooks, pencils, biros, make-up, tampons, keys, sandwiches, apples, mints, paper handkerchiefs, *The Pursuit of Love, Shorthand Practice,* the missing card. The constable noted everything with professional interest, only remarking, "A good thing we don't keep our warrant cards in our handbags."

The press seats were already full. They squeezed into the public benches, taking turns to fetch pages of copy from Devi, one of the agency's senior reporters, and dictate them to Fleet Street from telephone boxes outside.

Next day the case was held up by legal discussions. They sat for the first hour in another court, where the stipendiary magistrate worked at high speed through the routine list of overnight drunks, market lorries 'obstructing', prostitutes loitering. Then the not guilty pleas. Two men were offered interpreters, but shook their heads. The first, a gloomy little Italian, accused two women of stopping him and snatching his wallet, in one of those streets where as Browning put it 'sportive ladies leave their doors ajar.' All lies, they insisted: he was one of their regulars, he'd dropped the wallet upstairs, they were keeping it safe for him; they'd been shocked when the police turned up ..... The man listened with a bewildered expression, then turned to the magistrate:

"But, sir - I do not resort to such places. *I am a married man.*"

This simple remark seemed to take everyone aback. There was a moment's dead silence. Then the magistrate recited quietly:

"Who steals my purse steals trash ...
But he that filches from me my good name
Robs me of that which not enriches him
And leaves me poor indeed."

Then: "Case proved. Anything known about the defendants?"

Yes indeed. A long string of similar convictions.

Then came a genial Swede who had accosted an office cleaner on her way to work at dawn. She took the oath in fierce tones; needlessly, as he then explained that he wished after all to plead guilty.

The witness snapped, "I should think so too. Who does he think he is? He can't talk to respectable people like that."

The man bowed and said earnestly, "If you please I wish to apologise. You see, I did not take her for a respectable person. I took her for a prostitute."

On her face, outrage gave way to stupefaction. She stood open-mouthed. Kindly hands helped her from the box. All unaware of further offence, the visitor went off to pay his fine. Sarah murmured, "And the moral of that is - *never explain.*"

His place was taken by a student said to have used obscene language ' to the annoyance of passers-by.' This he denied: "I was quoting from *Ulysses.*" Case dismissed; also the next; a young girl, a suspected drunk, had been arrested while she was 'staggering about' in Downing Street. Sweetly she told the magistrate, "I don't drink. And I wasn't staggering. I was dancing. I was happy, that's all."

Outside, in the late afternoon, the air smelled of last night's lilac and early strawberries, though the great market stood empty. Rowan thought of a Whit Monday long ago, when she and her Aunt Lizard had gone strawberry-picking on a farm somewhere near the New Forest. She remembered endless rows of green and scarlet; cuckoos calling, toads sheltering under the leaves, and over it all the hot sweet fume of strawberry juice. A happy day, one of many with that favourite aunt.

Lizzie, a painter and traveller, had always been an ally. Last year, when she'd suddenly married Uncle Rollo (and high time too, Mother implied: they'd been in love for ages) and gone off with him to New Zealand, Rowan felt bereaved; but not for long. Their alliance seemed to work almost as well from there as from Lizzie's old studio in Chelsea, a few streets away from Rowan's home. It was to Lizzie and Rollo, a newspaperman, that she and Sarah owed their jobs.

Rollo, hearing that Rowan wanted to be a journalist, had written to Alex, a former colleague who now ran a court reporting agency, asking if she and her school friend might go with him to hear some cases in the Christmas holidays. One morning Sarah and Rowan had been left alone in a court where remands were being dealt with. One was a case of attempted murder. It would be remanded again, Alex told them. Would they let him know if a date were fixed for the hearing?

As they waited for the magistrates, a court officer put a labelled object on a table near by. A hatchet; actually showing dark red stains and wisps of grey hair mixed with dried blood. Then a young man in army uniform was brought in. The clerk read out his name: "You are charged that on such a date you did attempt to murder Daisy Ellen, your mother. And you are further charged that on the same date you did cause grievous bodily harm to the said Daisy Ellen ..."

A police inspector began to outline the case for the prosecution. The man in the dock was doing his national service. He came home on his first leave to find that his widowed mother had taken to spending her evenings in the public house ...

Sarah and Rowan looked at each other in doubt, then in alarm. The case wasn't 'going over' at all. Surely this *was* the first hearing? So - should they rush to find Alex? But he was busy in another court. So were the other reporters; and meanwhile the story was unfolding. They grabbed copy paper from the ledge under the press desk and began to scribble.

The accused had come home on embarkation leave before being sent to Cyprus. On his last evening at home his mother had left the house at six o'clock. At midnight he found her lying unconscious in a gutter. With the help of passers-by he carried her home. Two hours later he arrived at a police station to say that he had killed her with a hatchet, exhibit A, kept in the kitchen for chopping firewood. "I just felt I couldn't go off abroad," he'd said, "and leave her alone in that state."

In fact, despite terrible injuries, she had survived. Now she sat in a chair by the witness box, frail, and trembling, crying quietly, answering questions in hoarse reluctant whispers, while the clerk typed out her replies.

One of the reporters, Mike, arriving breathlessly several witnesses later, found that between them the novices had taken down most of the evidence. He had only to help them put it together for the late lunchtime editions. The case was being sent for trial at London Sessions.

"Oh, what will they do to him?"

"Depends. Poor devil. Might even find himself in Cyprus after all."

Their success was taken for granted, with flattering matter-of-factness, by the others. Later, Mike said, "Why not have a go at shorthand? Always useful you know." And Alex, saying goodbye at the end of the holidays, told them they were welcome to come in on Saturday mornings and lend a hand. And - by the way - he'd be wanting two new juniors in the spring.

Sarah and Rowan embarked on evening shorthand classes, and on a campaign to leave school straight away.

This was much easier for Sarah, who was already away from home, living with her married sister Caro on the other side of London. Rowan, an only child, still in the midst of family life, had to battle with dismay and disapproval. She'd been expected to stay two years in the sixth form and try for a university place.

"You don't know what you want! You're far too young to decide!"

But she did know; and had known for the past two years. She wanted to get a job, save up the fare and go out to New Zealand, and meet her cousin Ralph again - Rollo's son, a naturalist, who had been working out there for eighteen months and would probably stay on, like his father and Lizzie. And she must go soon - before it was too late, before he married someone else. (Or before the Bomb: as one must always say nowadays).

This resolve was too heartfelt, the outcome far too much in doubt, to be called a plan; and to mention it to another soul would of course be out of the question. She mustn't even think much about it beforehand. But their talk of being too young was simply absurd. The years were flying. Eighteen next birthday ... and Ralph would soon be *twenty-six*.

At school one day there was a folk song recital. Afterwards, one old ballad - a girl's lament for her lover 'beyond the seas' - went on humming in her mind.

"All round my hat I will wear the green willow

All round my hat for a twelvemonth and a day ..."

To her it was not a lament but a pledge. A year and a day after starting work, she promised herself, she would be ready to leave for New Zealand.

9

As for what might happen next - perhaps a love affair, perhaps marrying, having children, bringing them up in the rain forests - all that seemed immeasurably remote and incredible. An honour one might just occasionally dream of - Juliet of course was only pretending she hadn't, but then she was talking to her mother at the time - but still the sort of felicity one could imagine as coming true only for other people.

Sarah, for one. Beautiful even in the upper fourth and enviably self possessed, she now collected men of all ages wherever she went. And her sister Caro was always on her side; while Rowan's parents saw her as a child still, difficult and far from satisfactory.

Despite all this opposition, Saturdays in their last term were spent in the courts. And when other young people appeared there, brought by their parents as beyond control, they could picture all too well the scenes that had led to this drastic step.

One girl, fourteen, looking five years older, had been asked to leave her boarding-school because she'd climbed out at night in search of adventures. At home she did the same, hitching lifts into the outer suburbs, chatting up lorry drivers in roadside cafés, trying to persuade them to take her on long journeys; sometimes staying away for days. Brought back by the police, she simply watched her chance to be off again.

An order was made: for her own protection, the chairman patiently explained. Until she was sixteen, she was to stay in a house in the country, a place of safety for girls 'at risk'. There she would have good teaching, playing fields, a swimming pool, everything a girl could wish for - except the one thing she was interested in : men. She'd merely exchanged one boarding-school for another.

And would she really change? Go back to childhood, forget about sex, begin to study, to want a safer career than the one she'd embarked on - defiance, excitement, perilous new encounters, abortions, or bringing up babies in squalor 'on the welfare?'

Well, she might. Perhaps she'd had her fling, enjoyed shocking her relations, seen enough to know when to stop. But Rowan found herself wishing that her own parents could be in court to hear this; or the next application, from a widow trapped with a violent son of thirteen; or the near hysterical mother, with an absentee husband and three teen-aged girls, who complained that the middle daughter was destroying the family life; given to insane rages, when she would hit out, smash furniture, set fire to curtains, scream and rave, throw herself on the floor and tear the carpet with her teeth ... The magistrates listened, their faces impassive. And slowly another picture seemed to take shape, an eerie palimpsest: a glimpse perhaps of the real victim, the odd one out, picked on incessantly by the mother and sisters, driven to feelings she couldn't control, to rage, guilt, heartbreak, desperation?

Whatever the truth of that, Sarah and Rowan agreed that their own parents, and those of their school friends, so ready to find fault with sons and daughters in their teens, really led remarkably sheltered lives and had no idea what they were spared.

Not many misfits had Sarah's luck. Three years earlier, deeply unhappy at home, she had found refuge with Caro and her husband. Most people, old and young, just had to stick it out together.

4.

For Rowan the worst row of the final term had nothing to do with leaving school; or not outwardly. One evening she'd gone with Father to a film; always a doubtful pleasure, as he was easily bored and apt to keep up a flow of embarrassing comments, all too audible. As they sat through the advertisements - one for a local hairdresser's, showing matronly coiffures - he produced the kind of joke she dreaded: "Why don't *you* go there? - then you might look presentable for once." One or two heads turned curiously in their direction. Rowan, thankful for the dark, felt like Elizabeth Bennet that years of happiness couldn't make up for such moments of family life.

Next day, coming home from school, she found herself passing a different sort of hairdresser's, and on impulse went in and had her long straight hair cut off. The 'urchin cut', short and spiky, was still approved in the sixth. At home, as she'd foreseen, it produced an explosion: dismay from Mother, disgust from Father, icy remarks from both.

Queer, how families seemed to get worked up about *hair* ... Later, when tempers cooled, Mother began to laugh about it, recalling a time when she and Aunt Lizard and Aunt Rose all had their hair 'bobbed' in London - years later than most English girls they knew - and then had gone home to Ireland and been told by Grandfather that they weren't fit to be seen. And Rose had said calmly that he wouldn't have to see *her* much longer, she was marrying Rollo Oliver and going out with him to China, he'd been engaged by the *North China Daily Post.*

Rowan had no chance of escaping to China, where poor Aunt Rose had died long ago, leaving her small boy Ralph to be brought up by Aunt Lizard. But within a month her life had changed almost as dramatically. Grandfather had a mild stroke. Mother went over to Nine Wells, the family farm in Ireland, to help look after him. Father joined her, and stayed a week; and had then come home to tell Rowan of a startling new plan. He was going to retire almost at once from his job in the City; he and Mother would live in future at Nine Wells and run the place for the old people.

And Rowan?

It seemed that the hair-cutting had been - not a childish act of defiance - but a turning-point, a step towards independence. She hadn't made a mistake after all: the gamine look suited her. Both parents tacitly admitted as much. Now they went further, and agreed to her staying in London to work for Alex. Sarah would be taken on as well: "Let them come here for a start," he'd said, "then they'll want to begin applying to local papers."

Everything fell smoothly into place. Caro invited her to stay with Sarah. Her husband Breck worked for television news and was often away; she'd be glad of the girls' company, she told Mother.

Rowan, on her first visit to their home in Highgate, was ready to like any new lodging, and thrilled at what she found. The roomy late Victorian house, passed on from Breck's parents, stood on the crest of a long hill, surrounded by trees and gardens, with a distant view of green playing fields. It was of course too large for a young couple; but they meant to fill it with their children. Rowan's high attic room, next to Sarah's, looked down over budding treetops at the back of the house, with no building in sight except for a distant church spire. The long garden sloped down to a little wood where tawny owls lived in a hollow tree.

In her room at home she'd felt often, as someone or other had said, that she couldn't sleep at night 'for the desire of living.' She knew she would sleep soundly here, now that living was going to begin.

5

At school there was a distinctly chilly interview with the Head.

"Why be in such a hurry? Why not get some education first?"

One could always go on reading, Rowan offered.

"Oh, ... reading yes ... But there's more than that to university life. You're missing a great opportunity. Mixing with civilised people ... a chance to meet your intellectual superiors ..."

"We'll be mixing with journalists. Some of them seem quite civilised." In Sarah's little smiling voice this sounded innocent rather than impertinent. The Head smiled back forbearingly.

"Bet she doesn't know any," Sarah said afterwards. "Pity she can't meet - "

"Yeees ... who?"

"Well ... Derry Gillespie." They relapsed into giggles, remembering Derry, met in the holidays at Sessions; ace crime man, now ex-ace, sacked regretfully from several national papers, fended off by the rest: missing far too often in the Prince of This, The Duke of That. Now he worked odd days for the court agencies. But after an hour or so he would grow restless, slipping out with a whispered - "Shan't be long. Take a note for me, would you?" Dear old Derry, fifty at least, perhaps even more, but still like an engaging schoolboy; bright-eyed and curly-haired, funny and friendly, and full of tales about the crimes and corpses of a working lifetime, bodies in trunks, bodies burned in cars or buried in woods, dentures and other relics in acid baths, grim packages found at dawn on lonely marshes; screams in hotel bedrooms, plausibly explained. Not exactly the Head's idea of a civilised acquaintance?

Yet even Derry could be surprising.

One morning, in their first week as juniors, a new friend of Sarah's - Kim Spring, an up and coming young barrister - greeted her with -

"Well well. Here you sit like vultures, gloating over other people's misfortunes-"

"Ho, we're not here for that. We're here to see *you* don't get above yourselves." Derry, roused from one of his cat naps, said to Rowan,

"He's got a point, you know. Who were those chaps in the old days - church courts - took bribes? Sold pardons? And some Pope or other said - *They eat and drink the sins of the people.* And so do we. What?"

Taken aback, Rowan protested, "But what about lawyers? And judges? And the police? It's their living too!"

"Ah no. They're here to help. Guardians of the law. Not the same sort of thing at all ... oh well. Better than working as they say."

He squinted up at the clock, muttered "Time for matins," and edged sideways out of the high narrow press seat. On his way to the door he turned back, looking up at Rowan from below, and said in a different tone,

"But your little friend has a point too. People say - you'll hear it often enough - there ought to be *trained observers* in the courts. Keeping a check on the system. But where are they to come from? Who's to choose them and train them and pay them? What?"

"I don't - "

"Yes, well. They're here already. The press, no less. So don't you stand for that cant about vultures. Anyway," he added, half to himself, "we're just as likely as anyone to turn up in the list."

Rowan blushed. Derry, she knew, had been more than once in the morning queue at Bow Street, 'found drunk'. Sometimes at his own request. "If you start to pass out," he would advise, "hang on to your wallet and yell for the police."

"Silence! Be upstanding in court!"

"Oh Jesus," he muttered, making off. "Take a note, angel?"

She remembered Mike's tip about another old-timer, a high handed character who would spend his mornings elsewhere, then expect the young to be flattered by demands for copy. Wasn't that more or less what Derry did? Yet no one dreamed of resenting it. Other newsmen treated him as a kind of celebrity, quoting his exploits, past and present, as part of Fleet Street legend.

6.

So here she was: out in the world, grown up, and mixing with grown up people. She seemed to look back from a great distance at earlier contacts.

Vesy, for instance. Hard to realise that all that had been only the term before last.

He and Rowan had met on the train to school and drifted into friendship. An earnest sixth-former, he had recently discovered communism and required a listener for his lectures on its virtues, the evils and absurdities of all other political systems, the need for everyone to forgo any personal aims and ambitions, except in so far as they might contribute to the good of the Party. To celebrate this discovery he had changed his name, Vincent, to a Russian version, found in *War and Peace*. Russia, he explained, far from being a threat to the world, was the leader and light-bringer.

His own family remained unconverted, his older brothers cheerfully derisive, his parents concerned only with the effect on his exam results. Rowan too had to admit to herself that she felt no urge towards such an unselfish course; but Vesy never discovered this. All through November and December, school journeys and Saturday afternoons were taken up by her indoctrination; broken off almost absently, in cinemas, by inexpert kisses. In the Christmas holidays he was away, but more theses arrived daily in bulging envelopes, addressed without prefix to 'Rowan Dane,' so that Father felt driven to comment, "So this friend's a Friend, is he? A Quaker? No Misters or Misses?" and Rowan to retort, "No, not a Friend. A Comrade." "Oh God."

Proud to be thought worthy of such clever serious letters (so different from the curt What-about-Saturday? schoolboy notes that had so far come her way) Rowan showed some pages of political argument and social indignation to Mother, who found them touching, but was too tactful to say so, remarking instead, "He sounds a very nice thoughtful boy." A damning verdict, like all parental approval. But then the letters ceased abruptly. When term started he no longer waited for her on the tube platform or in their usual coffee bar. No explanations: he'd simply gone off her, she supposed, or found someone more politically minded.

Accepting this, not without a pang or two, she found the train seat beside her taken one morning by another sixth-former whom she knew by sight. His opening gambit was,

"Ever seen a painting by Denton Welch - young lady looking woebegone?"

"Don't think so. Denton who?"

"The title is - *Now I have only my dog.*"

Was she really looking like that? But she couldn't help laughing. He followed up his success with another - "'I would I were thy dog.'"

16

They were all doing "Romeo and Juliet." She found this quip brilliant, and deeply consoling; and that mannered style was impressive. It was her first experience of a changeover: she was reminded in secret of a time when a neighbour at home had lost her cat, and another had arrived on her doorstep, ready to fill the vacancy.

When she and Vesy met, unavoidably, he would colour and look away, and find a seat by another girl. All this was noted by Sarah, who knew his older brothers. She did a little research, and presently reported.

"You know what happened? It was all a tease, Tom and Giles found him writing to you, and they read the letter and pretended to be horrified, they said whatever was he playing at? - if he kept writing every day like that you'd think you were *engaged*, he'd find himself in a ghastly fix. And so on. And he believed them!"

"He can't have!"

"Well, men are always scared of getting trapped. Wouldn't you be if you were a man?"

Such encounters, of course, were mere pastime; nothing to do with her dream of the future. And already the future had begun to take shape, with Saturdays in the courts, evenings at shorthand and typing classes; and then her successful démarche at the hairdresser's. She regretted, however, that that lively row had coincided with a notice from school about a form trip to Paris in March. Last term, when this first came up, she'd been allowed to put her name on the list. Now Father said she didn't deserve it. Paris was definitely off.

But then, at the very last moment, it was on again.

7

Aunt Lizard, as so often, was the catalyst. On the morning when the form party was to leave, a letter arrived from her: would Rowan please help?

Lizzie was doing black and white decorations for a new anthology of English wildflower poems; her drawings showed the flowers in authentic settings. Most of her research had been done before she left, but last spring she'd had to miss two important journeys: to the Lakes for those daffodils, and to Oxford for Matthew Arnold's fritillaries.

Rowan was to go to a camera shop near Chancery Lane, and buy a little camera, and a couple of films. Then, in the Easter holidays, perhaps she could spare a day or two to visit Ullswater and take photographs? She would find exactly where and when in Dorothy Wordworth's Journal. A cheque was enclosed for expenses; and anything over was to pay her for her work.

The cheque was for fifty pounds. *Fifty pounds.* So there'd be a good deal over? Rowan looked at it in sheer disbelief. Then she handed the letter and cheque to Father across the breakfast table, saying from bravado,

"I suppose I could go to Paris now. Paying for myself."

Mother was still away at Nine Wells. Father, his mind full of plans for the removal, only glanced and said absently,

"Surely it's too late for that?"

"Someone's dropped out ... I could catch them at Victoria, and see -"

He sighed and looked down at his own letters.

"Only," she persisted, hope rising, "what do I do with that cheque?"

"Oh. Well. We'll see ..."

"But they're leaving *now*! This morning! I'd have to *rush* -"

To have her safely out of his way for a week ... perhaps that was the deciding factor. He got up, stalked into his own room and came back with a wad of notes.

"There you are then. Don't forget your passport. And ring me if you *are* going, of course."

Trembling with hope and excitement, she packed, found the passport, rang Sarah with a message for their form mistress, dashed after a bus, than hailed a taxi, taking one of those notes from its rubber band.

Then followed a rash and dream-like interlude.

At Victoria, checking Continental Departures, she saw Dover-Calais-Paris. And underneath: Dover-Calais-Basel-Milan-Florence.

Oh Florence, she thought with longing: shall I ever go there?

And then it flashed across her mind - I could, I could *now*. No one need know. Why not? Why not?

Alone? Without permission? Without telling anyone?

But he's let me go to Paris ... oh yes, with the school party. But I'd be all right. It's only a train and a boat and another train ... like going to

Ireland, and I've done that by myself. And then finding somewhere to stay - a *pensione,* wouldn't it be? - there must be plenty of those. And they say everyone speaks English. Oh, to be in Florence, like the Brownings (Robert's *Men and Women* was another of this year's set books) - to see where they lived with Penini, to see the Arno, and Fiesole, and the full moon lamping Samminiato, a hundred years on. To go where one liked, not tagging around with a lot of schoolgirls.

She walked slowly over to the other side of the station. There they were in the distance: Mademoiselle, and the other French mistress, and the chattering crowd, in school hats and raincoats like her own, waiting at the barrier. They hadn't seen her. She could just let them go. Why not?

It's my own money, now. I'm going to *earn* it.

And Father shouldn't have said 'She doesn't deserve it.' That wasn't fair. I deserve it as much as any of *them* ... even if that's not saying much.

She let them go. The dream had begun. She rang Father - "Just off. Yes, everything's fine. See you next Thursday -" her voice shook, her hand shook. The receiver clattered down, cutting her off. She thought calmly - Now I'm on my own.

She bought a ticket for Florence, changed some notes into beautiful lire, bought a phase book and sat in a quiet corner whispering: *Buon giorno, buona sera, per piacere, grazie, mi può dare una camera* - though not the kind she'd need for those daffodils, she thought, and laughed inwardly at this feeble joke, light-headed at the enormity of what she was doing. (But Lizzie would be on her side. So like her, coming up with all this lovely money, just at the right moment. And the Head was fond of saying 'Be adventurous.' One could quote that if there were trouble later.)

Once, when the waiting was almost over, she had a moment of doubt and nearly changed her mind, but not quite. Then she was in the afternoon train, rushing through sunny Kent, sailing out for the first time away from the harbour and the white cliffs, over a shining lavender sea. At Calais, a red misty sun was sinking, the stars came out, and she was no longer alone, but with a friendly pair of students, two years older, experienced travellers.

So it was all easy as well as breathtaking. From Basel they had a carriage to themselves, Nick and Sue entwined on one seat, fast asleep; Rowan stretched out on the other, wrapped in a warm mohair stole that Sue lent her; wide awake, gazing out at the snowbound landscape, deserted stations and eerie lamplight, dark forests, white peaks and precipices, frozen torrents hanging down rocks, fringed with jagged spikes of gold and silver ice. Through a sudden spectacular blizzard they came out into the dawn, with Monte Rosa pink-shadowed in the far distance. A brief pause: jaunty men in uniform skipped about with brisk cries of *Passaporte*; and then they were in Italy, in soft spring light, crossing the great plain: vast fields pale with March dust, outlined by slender budding trees, with here and there a tall narrow house, tinted cinnamon or apricot, a cloud of pink and white fruit blossom, a flourish of purple irises. On and on, hour after enchanting hour. And so to Florence, and a room in a dark narrow street, in the student lodgings where Nick and Sue were staying. One glimpse of Santa Maria Novella by twilight; then night and sleep, twelve hours of oblivion, and waking to her first Florentine morning, with sunlight flashing on the Arno.

There followed days of wandering, while her friends were at their lectures. The art treasures she could hardly attempt, they must wait for another time. Just now it was almost too much happiness simply to be here, ringed by domes and towers; to find that she was lodged near the same street as the Brownings on their first arrival; to dawdle by the river and remember a picture in the fifth-form room, Dante meeting Beatrice (and Beatrice so like Sarah, it might have been a portrait) and tell herself - it was *over there*; to cross the old bridge, so miraculously spared by the war, and find shabby haunted Casa Guidi, and wander up to Via Romana, then back and forth, followed everywhere by echoes of Browning, 'river and bridge and street and square'; to see glimpses of dark cypresses and flowering almonds behind high garden walls, and hear Italian blackbirds; to go by bus to Fiesole, then on the long ride to Vallombrosa, and more spellbound wandering; all this followed by heady evenings in crowded student caffès, delightfully tired and at ease, eating great mounds of pasta, drinking sour delicious wine, letting the babble of different accents ebb and flow around her, leaving her secret thoughts untouched.

Nick and Sue had pointed out at the start that in Italy, even in English school uniform, it was really best not to wander alone. An escort was found for her, someone's truant schoolboy brother, Mario. Rather piqued at being paired off with a fifteen-year-old, she soon realised all the same that she was lucky to have him, and let him practise his English in a day-long patronising monologue that recalled Vesy; though the subject was different, being chiefly a string of anecdotes about his love affairs, suitably toned down, as he implied. She let this flow over her with a tolerant smile; admitting to herself that - with his fine profile and olive skin, his great dark eyes, his cocky high spirits, and that engaging conceited tilt of the head - he was by far the most attractive boy she'd ever met.

All but one. If only Ralph could have been there with her ... some day perhaps?

She deliberately put off all nagging guilt and worry about her own truant situation; promising herself that, when she was home again, she'd tell her parents everything, and they'd see for themselves that - like Sarah - she had outgrown school journeys as well as school itself. To prepare them she sent off a postcard with a light-hearted message.

On her last morning she woke knowing herself exhausted, wrung out from sheer excess of feeling; and parched by this dry bright dusty southern spring, actually longing for rain and dewy green fields, thinking

20

with sudden insight - so that's what he meant by *O to be in England!* The discovery fired out her grief at leaving. The nearer she came to Calais, the stronger grew her pleasure at being homeward bound. She didn't care about the Force 8 gale in the Channel, the plunging rocking boat, the crowds of French schoolchildren, rowdy at first, then green-faced and ominously quiet. Dark skies were as welcome as the thought of rain-soaked Kentish orchards, budding elms and chaffinches.

The Paris party, thank heaven, weren't on this boat. No awkward meetings spoilt her return.

But later, as the train slid through damp south London, reaction set in. She woke to the fact that disaster might have struck. It had all seemed safe and simple, that morning at Victoria; and too remote to worry about, in Florence. But suppose it had come out that she wasn't with the school party? If so, it was serious. She'd been missing for days, they would all be frantic. Mother would have rushed home from Ireland. Her photograph might even have been in the newspapers.

She began to feel faint and sick; partly, she knew, from hunger and fatigue and travel pills, but also at the thought of what lay ahead. The more she went over it, the more likely it seemed that the worst might have happened.

Then she tried to reassure herself. Father, after her call from Victoria, would have taken for granted that she was with the others. Her form mistress, on getting Sarah's message, might have mentioned it to someone; but the chances were that she'd seen no need, that there'd been no follow-up, no alarm ... And she'd shown her passport just now at Dover, and no one had hailed her as the missing schoolgirl. Besides, she'd sent home that postcard: so by now they knew where she had really gone. There was only another family scene to be faced. And they'd have to admit that she'd managed very well on her own.

But, the closer that reckoning came, the more fervently she wished it needn't happen. If only she could just slip in quietly, to a bath and tea and toast; then fall into bed and sleep in peace, and dream of Italy.

8

And that was exactly what she did.

Her homecoming was a blessed anticlimax. There had been no need, after all, for that hour of dread and panic. No fatal disclosure, no disaster ... Mother was home, but only to start the business of removal. Enquiries about her trip were easily put off. "Yes, super. Tell you later. Too tired now." No one mentioned her postcard, for a simple reason: it hadn't arrived.

It came next morning; and with it another letter from Aunt Lizard, with news that eclipsed all other topics for the rest of the day. Staggering news. She'd actually had a baby. A son, Rufus. A miracle child, born in her forties, like Elizabeth Barrett Browning's.

In the flurry of talk and excitement - for Lizzie had given no hint of this beforehand - Rowan slipped the postcard into her pocket. They hadn't even seen it, let alone had a chance to notice the wrong stamp, wrong postmark, wrong river ... She could go off to school, scot-free. Perhaps no one but Sarah need ever know the truth.

Later, told about Lizzie's baby, Sarah asked, "What made her leave it so long, I wonder?"

"Oh well. When my cousin and I were young, she had *us*. We were like hers in a way. But now we're grown up ... and anyway, it must have been now or never."

"I suppose so. How old did you say she is?"

"Forty-five, Mother said. Pretty old to have a baby."

Sarah gave her on odd look. "Shall I tell you something? Caro's afraid she'll never have one. And she's only twenty-four."

"But - that's not old! She's got years -"

"Yes, but they've been married five years. Not a hope, so far."

"But - why? I thought, if people *wanted* one, it was simple?"

"So did I ... And she's had all sorts of check-ups. Nothing wrong, they told her. No use though."

"How *awful*."

"Mm. Don't let on I've -"

"As if I would!"

9.

Wordsworth's daffodils - her first commission for Lizzie - came as a surprise. She'd always pictured a mass of large yellow trumpets, King Alfred or Sir Watkin, tossing on a flat grass verge under a grove of high trees. In April, on one of those dewy mornings that Browning had Home Thoughts about, she put her bicycle on the train at Euston and sat for three hours looking out at miles of yellow gorse and spring wheat, hemmed in by spreading towns; then, on a long slope before Penrith, looking down into rooks' nests in swaying treetops, and over to the far mountains, their peaks still touched with snow. From Penrith she set out for Ullswater, taking a roundabout route to visit Grasmere. Mother had wanted to book her a room somewhere for the night, but she'd preferred finding one for herself in a youth hostel or farmhouse. Dazzled by the grandeur of lakes and mountains, she put this off, and went on and on until darkness fell, then turned into the first hotel she came to. It was full; but a fatherly porter told her she might have dinner there and sleep at a nearby cottage where his mother lived.

In a little bare room with dark beams and a tiny window full of starlight, sunk in a deep feather bed, she dreamed she was sleeping in Dove Cottage. At dawn she crept out through the kitchen, leaving money on the table beside a sleeping cat, and cycled through still mist to the grey stormy lake. There, in a wood of young birches and sallows, she saw what she had come for: drifts of tiny wild daffodils, clustered among ferns and mossy stones, surely the very stones that William and Dorothy had seen a century and a half ago; with here and there a violet or celandine, their leaves glossy with rain, or white with hailstones like wood-sorrel buds.

No hope of taking photographs. Black clouds hid the sun; then a violent hailstorm drove her to shelter in another hotel. The prospect seemed bleak, her expedition wasted. Yet even in this gloomy interlude, with frozen rain rattling on the windows and squalls whirling across the lake, she was captivated by these wild surroundings, wondering why she lived in London and whether she need stay there for another year.

But soon she was too busy to pursue this train of thought. The clouds blew away, the birds sang, sunlight glittered on the water; the little daffodils lifted their heads again from drifts of melting hailstones. She took a dozen photographs, promised herself a return, and set off for home.

But home, of course, was no longer what it had been.

She and Sarah were to start work in mid-April; and then the move to Ireland would take place. A month was spent in dismantling, discarding, packing. People came every day to 'view' the flat; then the buyers, two or three times more, to measure and plan.

Some day, Rowan thought, there might be time to look back with nostalgia at her early years at the top of this tall elegant town house; to regret its loss, and the takeover by strangers. Now, keyed up and restless, she was simply impatient to be done with all the fuss, to shake off the past and begin her new career.

Not precisely, she realised, a life of independence; or not yet. Father would pay rent and board to Caro. She would have £5 a week from Alex, but she'd need all this, they told her, for day to day expenses, and to buy new clothes. Meanwhile, Mother chose her a neat fawn suit and girlish blouse, and would have added a hat, but Rowan protested too vehemently. As it was, when she appeared at breakfast on their first morning, Sarah grinned and said,

"Porridge colour ... h'm, very tasteful. A bit director's-secretary, though?" Sarah was wearing a little scarlet jacket, with her black ballet skirt and sleeveless jersey. She lent Rowan some garments of the same kind, suitable for jiving after work.

They were sent to court that day with the youngest reporter, Toby, to collect an 'ordered case' from among the drunks. An unlucky clergyman, up for a night from his country parish, had dined too well at a friend's house, sat on a low wall outside to recover, and unwisely snapped "Oh, go away," when a policeman spoke to him.

Fined forty shillings. Toby and Sarah went off to the press room, Rowan stayed to watch for more snippets for the evening papers.

Today the public seats were filled with a party from a Townswomen's Guild. The magistrate, never one to waste an audience, set out to entertain them. A market man, fined for obstructing the highway, protested, "I shall never live to pay, I am dying." "Oh, I do hope not, Mr. Fleury. You're one of our best customers." The man was not amused. (And Rowan wondered - how do *we* know what a doctor might have told him?) The next took his cue alertly: "Ho, we are all merry and bright today." Two street card tricksters made a routine appearance, together with the routine witness, a police sergeant who spent much of his working life on the tops of buses. From there he had a good view of operations - the cards spread out on a coat, the ring of gullible passers-by - and was sometimes quick enough to reach the scene before the players were tipped off and vanished. The magistrate had him into the box to explain the ancient lure of Find-the-lady. Then came a shaggy youth in a tattered sweater: for begging and handling stolen goods. "I wasn't begging, I was collecting for the poor and unemployed." "You and your mates?" "Well, I gave everyone a book. That's a sale, not begging." The books were pamphlets on Yoga, missing from a shop in the Charing Cross Road. "I found them in a toilet." 'Nothing known' (no previous convictions). He was bound over to be of good behaviour.

Then a list of prostitutes loitering, usually fined "Forty shillings or one day," the 'day' being served by the time the court rose for lunch. Sometimes, if a larger fine were imposed, the girl would send out for the money, being detained until it arrived. Legend had it that in one such case the magistrate, by-passing these explanations, had said absently, "Well, see what you can do by lunch-time" - raising more grins in court than he'd bargained for.

At one point he had a brisk sotto voce argument with the clerk, and announced skittishly, "I might get into trouble with the Solicitor-General - not that I care!" A pause; then he leaned down from his high seat. "I should like to speak to the press."

Glancing right and left along the empty seat, it dawned on Rowan - the press is *me*. She jumped up, feeling conspicuous as Alice (*All persons more than a mile high to leave the court*) and he beamed at her over his spectacles: "Shall we forget that bit about the Solicitor-General?"

That idea of flight from London had soon receded, then vanished, blotted out by the pace of life. Only now and again there were reminders of past Aprils in Ireland. One soft breezy day, hurrying to a court through a narrow crowded street, smelling petrol, grime, sweaty clothes, cheap scent, fried onions, she thought - if only one could smell spring flowers instead, primroses, violets, just once more, before they're over! Turning back to the flower-sellers by the tube, she came to a barrow heaped with purple and labelled, yes, Devon Violets; caught up a bunch, and exclaimed, "Oh - but they're *violas*!" Summer flowers. The seller, taking her shilling, agreed, "That's right, love, I can't spell." But then, far down the next street, she saw a little gnome-like man lounging against the wall, balancing a tray of flowers, pale yellow ringed with green leaves. Another cheat, another illusion? He watched her approach, a faint expectant grin on his face, as though he'd been waiting for her: as though she'd *called him up.* This time the primroses stayed primroses. She tipped all the money out of her purse.

May was warm and sunny, by June a heat wave had set in. Court buildings were sealed closely for security; air conditioning lay in the future. Judges and barristers suffered in wigs and gowns, pressmen in tweed jackets. The girls, in their sleeveless cotton dresses, were envied.

Up at Highgate, in the early mornings, a glossy pair of mallard sometimes perched above the tube entrance, looking down curiously at the crowds of humans pouring underground. In the evenings, coming back from below, returning toilers found air cooled by light sea winds from the distant estuary. Caro would have a chicken roasting or a moussaka bubbling; if she and Breck were out, there would be appetising cold things in the fridge. After supper they took mugs of iced coffee down to the wild end of the garden and sat among bluebells and ragged robins, then foxgloves and blue cranesbill; listening to the chant of a hidden blackcap and waiting for the high summer stars. As darkness fell, a mother hedgehog would lead her young ones to breakfast on saucers of milk set out for them on the lawn.

On Saturdays, when the courts usually rose early, they would go shop-gazing, then to a dance club or jazz cellar with Mike and Toby, or to a Classic cinema, to some film made in their infancy or even before they were born; hearing Leslie Howard say 'Death that hath sucked the honey of thy breath Hath had no power yet upon thy beauty,' and Charles Laughton, 'I'll live to see you - all of you - hanging from the highest yard-arm -,' and Anna Neagle, 'Men are April when they woo, December when they wed,' and Jean-Louis Barrault, 'C'est tellement simple, l'amour,' and Roger Livesey, 'I am MacNeil of Kiloran. And I am the Laird of Kiloran' - as who should say, 'My name is Ozymandias, king of kings ...'

In those first weeks there was still a secret triumph in the thought that their school friends, with exams ahead, would be taking home piles of prep, while they were free to spend their leisure time as they pleased. Because of this sense of freedom, by tacit consent they would avoid walking past the vans in which the poor prisoners waited to be taken to Holloway or Brixton. But the thought of the prison van was not so easily shaken off.

One Saturday there was the case of a diplomat's ex-wife, now his widow, admitting fraud: she had ordered vast amounts of drink she couldn't pay for, to hold parties in a flat whose rent she couldn't pay either. The last party had been thrown to celebrate her ex-husband's death. Years before, when they were still married, he'd taken out life insurance in her favour: so hurrah, she thought, that would pay for the party champagne. But there was no insurance money after all. In court it came out that she'd been in this sort of trouble for years, had been through many county courts, the subject of countless medical and social reports, none of which was going to help her now. Well-groomed, well-mannered, politely detached, she sat looking blankly from one speaker to another, while magistrate and counsel conferred and sighed and tried to find a way out, but failed. This time it would have to be Holloway. And the idea of her in there, still looking polite and puzzled, facing months without a martini, spoiled the pleasure of the evening.

As so often, they wondered - what would become of her? Clearly she'd been sheltered all through her early life; someone had always been there to pay the bills. Now, alone and unsupervised, deaf to reason, she might end up like the little creature they'd found, early one morning, curled down in a sleeping-bag in the tube Ladies, with a bulging pack for a pillow. True, *she'd* seemed quite self-possessed; had merely opened one eye, winked at them in conspiracy, settled down for another nap. And at least she had her freedom; so long as she kept out of the social workers' clutches.

Besides ... it all depended on one's point of view. Another white-haired waif, unhappy in an old people's home, had gone up to a policeman on point duty in Oxford Street and asked him to arrest her so that she could go back to Holloway. She was lonely, she said, and she'd been happy in there. Plenty of company. When the officer laughed and sent her away, she'd found a brick and smashed a shop window, then went back to him in triumph: "Now you've *got* to nick me." Remanded for reports, to Holloway.

Caro was secretary to a consultant in Wimpole Street, and her work so confidential that she said very little about it; but when they met at supper she would encourage the girls to talk about their day. So did Breck if he were there. He of course moved in higher spheres, interviewing celebrities for television news; but he was very fond of Sarah, and intrigued by her progress from schoolgirl to working woman, and would draw her out and add anecdotes of his own novice days.

Like her sister, Caro was dark and graceful, but of a different type. Sarah was slim, lively and quick in all her ways; Caro taller, of larger build, quiet and self-contained. Her looks gave an immediate impression of warmth, good sense and balance; but, as Rowan came to know them better, she saw in Caro a kind of vagueness and uncertainty of manner which made Breck at times impatient and irritable. This loss of confidence, Sarah declared, was quite unlike her: "I do wish you'd known her a year or two back. Just not the same person ... she's got so *piano.*" The trouble was this baby problem, and the dreadful sense of failure.

Once, when she'd brought Sarah away from their family home, Caro had been anxious and protective on her sister's behalf. Now it was the other way round.

At fourteen, Sarah had been in love with an older boy, Richard, a school friend of her brothers, staying with the family while his parents were abroad. For a long time she had managed to keep her feelings secret. Then a smaller brother guessed, and betrayed her to the others. Caro rescued her from their teasing, and she had grown up in peace, waiting to meet Richard again at the proper time.

And now?

Sarah had admitted rather sadly, but laughing too - "Well, it all seems ... oh, just *myth*, you know. I don't even want to see him again. At least ... I don't care if I do or not. But," she added slowly after a moment, "It was real love, at the time."

Oh yes, Rowan thought. Real love. Mine too. And it still is.

Not every young married couple, Mother had impressed on Rowan, would be kind enough to share their home with two scatterbrained school leavers. But in fact the four of them got on admirably together; the more so, no doubt, because they were deeply absorbed in their own affairs, seeing little of each other, but enjoying their brief encounters. The only shadow came from Caro's situation, and the fact that Breck was so often away.

Then a blow fell. Caro told them despondently one evening that he was being sent to Cyprus with a camera team, to report on the troubles.

Sarah said quickly, "How long -?"

"Oh well. He *says* two or three months - but he might stay on. One man was abroad somewhere nine months, and then ..." Her voice trailed off.

And then - what? It was very dangerous out there; and not only for servicemen.

Later Rowan asked Sarah, "Does he have to go? Couldn't he get out of it?"

"Of *course* not, I expect he volunteered. He's dead keen, I mean frightfully keen. Rotten luck for Caro, though."

"Mm. Three months ."

"Or nine months -"

There was a long silence.

They were sitting together in the window of Sarah's attic, watching for the evening flight of two tawny owls. Far away the lights of Hornsey Lane shone; the vast space in between was filled with blue dusk.

Suddenly they exclaimed together - "There!"

The owls slipped out of the wood at the end of the garden and came winging upward, making for a gap between the houses, on their way to the oakwoods to begin their brief night's hunting. For a moment, in close-up, the watchers had a rare breathtaking glimpse of the two round soft faces, great eyes and soundless outstretched wings; then they were gone, and a bat began to flicker to and fro in front of the windows. A pale moth, fluttering by the glass, vanished like a speck of dust into a hoover.

Sarah said quietly, "You know what would be super? If Caro -" She paused.

Rowan nodded. No need to fill that pause.

If only she could start a baby *now*. And have it while Breck was away.

Rowan's second errand for Aunt Lizard was quite different from her lone bicycle ride in the Lake District. On a brilliant Sunday in May, a day of chestnut blossom, white hawthorn and darting swallows, Devi drove her to Oxford, with Mike and Sarah, to track down Matthew Arnold's fritillaries; he'd done this already, he said, as an undergraduate.

In Charing Cross Road, for a shilling, Rowan had picked up the Poetical Works, in sage green binding, inscribed To Flora, from Father, Christmas 1894. Searching through it on the way, she exclaimed, "Can't find them! Bluebells, orchises - no fritillaries - *isn't* it the Scholar-Gipsy?"

"Try Thyrsis," Devi advised.

"Oh . Yes ... 'the grassy harvest of the river-fields, Above by Ensham, down by Sandford ... ' What's this about the Arno vale, though?"

"His friend had just died. In Florence. Clough. You know - Say-not-the-struggle-nought-availeth."

"Oh. That one. Weird, isn't it," she added, still reading, "all this about flocks and pipes and simple country joys - those two! As though you and Mike were pretending to be shepherds!"

Mike said gently, "My father is a shepherd."

"No! A real one?"

"Quite real." He read over her shoulder," 'In reach of sheep-bells is my home'."

"Mine too, in Ireland. But then - what are you -?" she stopped short of an impulsive question. Devi finished for her,

" - doing in London, she means? 'The great town's harsh, heart-wearying roar?'"

"What a lot of us do, if we can. Getting the hell out of country life."

"Yes. I do see ... " Out of bleak dark winter days, toiling in rain and sleet and icy winds, mud and frost and dung; midnight lambing, coping with strays lost in snow-drifts, disgusting sheep diseases; living in a damp cottage, no amenities, no girls probably, nowhere to go on winter evenings; and all for a fairly slender wage.

Mike said suddenly - "You remember that poem of Hardy's, about Christmas Eve, and the oxen kneeling? When we read that at school I couldn't bear it, I felt quite mad with boredom, sort of stuck in the past, I wanted to live *now* ... Funny, though," he added, after a moment's thought. "Last Christmas I heard Robert Donat reading it on the radio - and I didn't mind any more. I quite liked it."

"And ... do you ever go back?"

"Most Sundays," he admitted. "By train. Through Adlestrop, by the way. Would your aunt like us to go there next?"

Their own Sundays as a rule were spent at home, at the grassy end of the garden. The lawn was part of an ancient sheep-walk, the crisp turf scattered over with daisies, white clover, lady's-fingers and thyme. After a flurry of laundering and shoe- cleaning they would lie there all day enjoying the sun and air; a respite from the stifling climate of the courts.

In the late afternoons, as the heat wave grew fiercer, press cellars held scarcely a mouthful of air; smoke battled with the smell of drains. The din of typewriters echoed from wall to wall. Copytakers at the other end of telephones were even crosser than usual:

"What a filthy racket - can't hear a word. Not that it matters. Who's going to use crap like this?"

Frustrated reporters, Alex would say charitably; and the girls, knowing their own good luck, tried not to snap back.

Times copytakers, after this, would take them by surprise with their amiable politeness. Only one other typist could match them: a veteran on a more frivolous paper, cheerful, brisk, never at a loss:

" ... works by Berthe Morisot, Sisley, Cuyp and Delacroix," one might read, after a spelling check with a newspaper library. Or -

" ... born in Zloczow, childhood in Machynlleth, emigrated to Toowoomba -" and the voice would murmur, "Yes? - yes? - yes? -" - his typewriter ticking on without a moment's check.

Then there was a strike; copy had to be delivered by hand. On blazing afternoons they escaped to scurry up and down shady byways off Fleet Street, handing out packets to chatty men in glass boxes; except in Printing House Square, where a haughty personage, like a butler in a ducal household, waved them away in disdain from the front portals to a kind of tradesmen's entrance at the back.

On a day of close oppressive heat a dozen boys and girls appeared in court together, accused of obstructing a policeman in the execution of his duty. They had been idling one spring afternoon outside a coffee bar, and the constable, a youth of about their own age, had told them to move on. They refused, saying they weren't obstructing anyone or breaking any law. It had all been trifling enough at first, but then the arguments grew heated, more police were sent for, scuffles began and arrests were made. Now they were answering to bail, and their friends rallied to their support. A hundred or more came pouring through the front doors, packing the public seats in court or waiting outside; all dressed in tight trousers, or grubby dark sweaters and ragged jeans, the uniforms of the moment. Already the atmosphere began to seem explosive.

The Bench filed in, trying to appear calm and tolerant; apprehensive, Rowan thought, was how they actually looked. By contrast, the clerk looked faintly quizzical. He was much younger than the magistrates, with oval face, high forehead, shrewd eyes; very like the First Folio Shakespeare portrait at school. The case might go for trial at Sessions; he prepared to type the evidence.

The twelve accused all pleaded not guilty. The constable told his story. It was received by defendants and onlookers in mutinous silence that underlined mounting tension. Clearly they'd all agreed, or been warned, to behave discreetly and give no excuse for the court to be cleared.

Only one of the twelve accused, acting as spokesman, chose to question the witness. He did this so skilfully that the young policeman was soon at a loss, blushing and stumbling, trying to hold firmly to his line but not quite a match for the questioner: who also, more surprisingly, knew when to stop. Senior officers, following him in the box, agreed that the twelve had in the end gone quietly to the police station and behaved there in an orderly manner. Again, as the prosecution ended, there was an ominous hush, like the stillness of boiling oil heated almost to flashpoint.

The spokesman was called first, went into the box and gave his name.

"And your address, please?"

"I have three addresses." For the first time, a note of boyish insolence. "Which do you want?"

The clerk said affably, "Yes? - May I have them all, please?"

They were given: Oxford, Oxted, Balls Pond Road. Yes, he was an undergraduate. Yes, he'd been outside the coffee bar. Yes, the first witness had asked them to move on ... the quiet courteous questioning went forward, the replies were tapped out on a typewriter. And minute by minute, in some mysterious way, the atmosphere changed. The heat was off, the simmering died down. By the time a third defendant reached the box, the Bench were allowing themselves an occasional cautious smile.

Then, quite soon, it was over. The magistrates, conferring together, not troubling to retire, nodded agreement: the case was dismissed. The chairman spoke of a misunderstanding, a storm in a coffee cup. "The police were quite right to bring these cases, but ..."

Slowly, in a haze of anticlimax, the audience drifted away, looking puzzled; cheated perhaps. It had all been quite different from what they'd expected. They appeared to have *won* ... and there had been no bullying, no unfairness. That guy with the typewriter had seemed - without doing a thing, except *ask*, and type - almost as if he'd been on their side.

No story either, except for the local paper.

Derry yawned - "Clever chap, that."

"The law student?"

"Oh, *him*. The clerk, I mean."

Yes: it had all been his doing. With a different type, elderly and irritable, there might have been a riot. Relaxed, disarming, good-humoured, he'd taken charge, reassured everyone, turned off the burner; kept the Queen's peace in fact.

"Police used to be like that," Derry added. "Now they're starting to get edgy."

In the next case, certainly, everyone had been pretty edgy. Plain-clothes police, hidden in a parked van, had kept watch for several days on a 'disorderly house.' An inspector said in evidence that they then arrived together on the doorstep, to be greeted tersely by madam. "I'm not having this crew in all at once."

"I told her I was a police officer and that I had a warrant for their arrest" (court language for *All you lot - down the nick*) and she had thrown a bowl of goldfish at him.

Poor goldfish. Had they been left to die, floundering and gasping?

Derry thought not. One of the squad would have scooped them up and dunked them in the sink. The police were still quite well disposed to animals; and as a rule, to the young:

"Cup of tea going, down by the cells."

"Oh thanks. What's the quickest way down to the cells?"

"Hit me in the face, love."

14.

When Breck arrived in Nicosia, Caro would hurry home each evening to switch on the television news, watching for glimpses of bomb damage, reports of attack and counter-attack, ambush, raids, shootings and explosions; getting up early to wait for the post. His letters, scribbled in some hotel bar, were brief and breezy, with an occasional offhand flourish - "Our car stoned again today" - or a libel on some charming overworked official: "You rush in to ask, What about this incident? - and he says, Oh my dear fellow, *another* incident? - and then tells you to go and see Aphrodite's Baths." But under it all one sensed the strain of living in a hostile country.

Despite her anxiety, Caro seemed at first resolutely cheerful. Then one evening they found her crying quietly into a cup of coffee.

To their frightened questions she would say only, "No, it's all right - *he's* all right - take no notice," before she escaped upstairs.

At bedtime Sarah confided, "She was late. She'd started hoping."

"No luck?"

"No luck." Sarah drummed on a window pane with her nails, muttered "Isn't it absolutely foul?" and lapsed into brooding silence.

Rowan looked down into the twilit garden. A perfect place for children. No pram on the lawn, though, on the long sunny days. No one to pick daisies, climb the apple trees, build secret houses in the wood.

Not, of course, that childhood always appeared in such idyllic guise; or motherhood either.

A pair of blackcaps had returned to the garden, to nest in a high clump of ivy beside the fence. All day a soft persistent warbling filled the air, as the cock bird roved from tree to tree, hidden among the leaves. They were there every summer, Caro said; but this year there was a hazard. Two noisy children had come to live in the house next door.

Should they tell them about the nest? Or - would it be safer to let the birds take their chance?

At length Caro called the two over, pointed out where the nest was, and begged them to play for the next few weeks on the other side of the garden. This seemed to go down well. Robin and Linnet were all agog. They gazed up at the ivy, bright eyed and compliant, nodding and promising.

Next day, for once, work finished early. Reaching home at tea-time, Sarah and Rowan heard a strange din outside the kitchen window. Below they saw Robin and Linnet, armed with sticks, beating on the fence, yelling at the tops of their voices and lobbing stones up into the ivy. As the window flew open, the onslaught stopped abruptly; the pair fled, giggling.

Caro said afterwards, "Well, that'll teach us. All the same - I've a good mind to tell their mother."

"No point. Is there? She'd never believe they did it on purpose." Their new neighbour, Beth Pringle, was a kind well-meaning creature, clearly no match for her offspring.

And it was too late to save the nest. The birds had deserted.

In court, to round off this ill-starred week, a man was accused of accosting small boys in the park. In the dock he seemed terrified and apologetic. The boys were so young that, when the first was put into the witness-box, the magistrate directed that his mother should stand beside him. Gently questioned, he told how they had been followed to and fro until they grew frightened and approached a policeman. Cross-examined, he denied trying to attract the man's attention. "No we never. We was just walking about. All the time he kept after us."

A second boy appeared, also with his mother, and told the same story. But then, questioned further, he began to fidget and look unhappy. Why hadn't they left the park? No reply. Yes, he admitted, he did know the man already. Yes, they'd seen him there before. Yes, he knew he'd been in trouble.

"What kind of trouble?"

The mask of innocence slipped, the childish pipe sank to a sullen undertone. "Took boys home."

When the third child was brought in, the magistrate again invited his mother to stand with him; but by now his tone had an edge of sarcasm. This time, counsel for the defence drew out a cruel story: a relentless game of hide and seek, then a game of hunt and kill. The mother stood, red-faced and grim, by the boy's side.

Case dismissed. The man in the dock began to sob.

A horrid shock for the mother, Rowan thought at first. But afterwards she wondered: was it? She was no Beth Pringle; had probably suspected the truth all along. Mightn't it in fact be just one more thing, the sort of thing she'd learned to expect from life?

At Sessions, earlier in the week, there had been an odd little scene in the court tea-room. Three attendants, sensible-looking middle-aged women, rather like that boy's mother, had been standing together at the counter, listening to a programme about weddings on a small radio. The sound was turned down to a discreet murmur so as not to disturb the only other tea drinker, a barrister at a distant table. He seemed engrossed in his papers. But then, as the organ rang out in a recording of some royal marriage service, he suddenly turned and began to harangue them bitterly.

"Weddings! What vile sentimental humbug! let me tell you, all that means to a man is a life sentence - mortgage, insurance, school fees, bills and more bills. God knows what else - a married man's at his wits' end just to exist, as often as not! *That's* marriage for you! And then what's to

37

happen if he falls ill? If he can't keep going on the treadmill? Enough to make any man cut his throat and have done with it all!"

He swallowed his tea, crashed his papers together and swept out with a last vindictive "Tcha!"

No one spoke. The women had waited with respectful impassive faces, showing no flicker of surprise. Now one of them put out her finger and turned up the sound. A choir was singing O Perfect Love. They settled down again to listen.

15.

One morning as Rowan passed the robing-room at Sessions the door opened and a barrister rushed out and stopped her. He was due in court, and in trouble: the strings that secured the white starched bands behind his high collar were knotted, and too loose; and he couldn't get the knot undone. Could she please have a try?

Rowan did so, thankful for the long finger-nails that would have been frowned on at school. That evening in the coffee bar she said doubtfully to Sarah, "Guess who's asked me to dinner? Arran Green. You know - with the beard and glasses -"

"What'? the mystery man? That looks like Lear?"

"He's not *that* old!"

"Not King. Owl-and-pusscat."

Sarah's barrister friend Kim Spring had told them about this character. Reputed brilliant, he appeared only rarely, when a brief took his fancy. Sarah was impressed. *"How pleasant to know Mr. Lear.* Since when?"

"This morning. He'd got knotted." She described their meeting. "Then the usher brought me this." An engraved card, with his name, an address in Hendon, and a scrawl on the back: Will you do me the honour of dining with me tonight?

"You'll do him the honour of course?"

"Oh well. I did say yes - but he's probably forgotten all about it."

"Rubbish. You simply must."

"Look, why don't you come too? I could ring and ask?"

"Of course not. Tactless -"

"I don't see why?"

"He'd think you thought he wasn't safe. May not be either."

"What, dear old Lear? D' you think so?"

"I can't anyway. Dinner at Schmidts."

"Kim again?"

"No, that one from the BBC. Mind you do go. Tell me later?"

Left alone, Rowan fought her panic. Could she possibly talk, all through dinner, to an elderly man ... as old as Derry perhaps ... a distinguished sophisticated stranger? Very different from bacon and eggs in Chelsea with Mike or Devi. It was all very well for Sarah, never shy or tongue-tied ...

But she saw that she must go. It would be cowardly not to. So she'd better stop worrying and just think about what to wear. For the first time in her life, she actually had a choice of brand new clothes. White jeans and black-and-white striped shirt? Or cream ballet skirt with scarlet pockets and matching top? The jeans, perhaps; and she'd take her mohair sweater as well, powder-blue, ravishing, her favourite garment. But then - with the skirt, she could wear her gipsy earrings? All the way home in the tube, and then on her way to Hendon, she fingered the card in her pocket and tried to pluck up her courage.

Long after dark she and Sarah met on the doorstep.

"So you did go! No, wait, don't tell me yet. I've got to eat. I'm starving ..."

"What? After Schmidts?"

"Only we never got there. Drinks all the way." She recited, "The George, The Sun and Horseshoe, The Earl Russell, Bear and Rummer, One Tun, The Cambridge - "

"You're making it up!" Rowan sank on to a chair in the kitchen.

"I'm not, I took a note, wait - Northumberland Arms, Hare's Foot, The Valiant Trooper -"

"No food at *all*?"

"Not a bite. Lots of talk though. And ten tomato juices, more or less. For me, I mean. Then I nipped off to Goodge Street tube, I bet he's never noticed."

"Too drunk?"

"Not drunk a bit, just thirsty. So how was Mr. Lear?"

Rowan said dreamily,

> "He lives in a beautiful lair-a
> With hundreds of books on the wall.
> He drinks a great deal of Madeira
> But never gets tipsy at all ...

I am, though. Quite. I think."

"Caro, quick, let's all have omelettes -"

"Not me," said Rowan. "I had a super dinner."

"Ah. Cooked by a wife? Housekeeper? A Bunter?"

"No, he cooked it himself."

"Oh. One of those. Haute cuisine?"

"Not haute at all. Just good. He lives alone. A sort of recluse. Not queer, I shouldn't think. You know ... ex-ex- (I am tight.) Eccentric, yes ... I liked him.. I like him."

"Touching, was he?"

"Oh shut up."

"And he didn't pounce?"

"Of *course* not. Not like that at all."

"Never crossed his mind?"

"Well ... perhaps. Then he thought better not."

Rowan fell silent, sipping black coffee.

It had been a strange evening.

She found the place easily enough; a block of mansion flats, quite imposing outside: wrought iron gates, white stone steps, brass door-knobs; red stair-carpet inside, and glossy banisters. On the first floor, answering her ring, he appeared in shirt-sleeves, a tea-cloth over his arm, a glass in his hand: not, as she'd feared, surprised to see her. Blue smoke poured from a little kitchen, and appetising smells - tarragon, black butter, onions frying. Left alone in his sitting-room with a glass of Madeira, the first she'd tasted, she had time to look about: dark solid furniture, leather armchairs, heavy velvet curtains, red and blue patterned carpet; the kind of setting one imagined for stories about West End clubs. But the details were less conventional. She noticed a light fur of dust everywhere; a regiment of old lead soldiers, their colours worn dim as though by much handling; a globe of the ancient world; an Oriental-looking sword; an Army jungle hat; a model of the Santa Maria; on the sideboard a pile of little bones - wishbones, knucklebones - dry and polished. On the hearth stood a large yellow bowl covered with a white cloth: bread rising, she knew from the faint yeasty smell - Grandmother always set her dough to rise by a warm hearth. Beside it stood two open wine bottles. (Two - so there must be other guests coming. Thank goodness - they'd do the talking.) Bookshelves covered three walls. From her armchair she made out various names: Saki, Sherlock Holmes, Agatha Christie, Suetonius, Thucydides, *The Great War between Athens and Sparta*; some in handsome bindings, but all, like the little soldiers, shabby with use. The shelves in front of the books were lined with household stores, bags of Strong White Flour, packets of yeast, glass jars of coffee beans, silvery garlic crowns, bunches of radishes, rows of Cox's pippins at all stages from green to golden brown.

A bachelor life-style. Everything useful and practical, or else valued for some reason; nothing *pretty* or just for show. She was fascinated.

He came in briskly, set down hot plates and drew out a chair for her. Only two places were laid, after all. He poured claret, dived back into the kitchen and returned with a sizzling grill pan. There were large steaks, crisp onion rings, tomatoes, mushrooms; an aromatic sauce. Another dish, smoking hot from the oven, held a kind of potato puff, pale brown, crisp and light. Then apple pie and cream. Stilton and celery, home-made bread, dark coffee.

And she needn't have worried about trying to talk. Sipping his way through the wine, he began to tell her the story of his life. A solitary only child, living in a world of his own, playing with his soldiers. Wanted to be a soldier first, then a surgeon. Made to read for the bar like his father. Then the war. He'd escaped into the Army, wanted to stay there afterwards, but ... on and on, vivid anecdote after anecdote ... the compulsive monologue of a solitary with a captive and captivated listener. (Why did this seem familiar? Yes, she remembered: Vesy, last year. And there had been Mario, in Florence. Different themes, but the same sort of eloquence.)

42

He used a good many unfamiliar words, and she tried to fix them in her memory (pejorative, metonymy, praxis) so as to look them up tomorrow; but they flashed past and were gone, like those eerie snowbound stations on her night ride through Switzerland, with names she could never catch (solipsism, symbiosis, eclectic, arcane). Long before she'd finished her first glass of claret, the evening had taken on something of the dream-like nature of that journey. The recital went on, the dream deepened. After a long time, they were sitting companionably, close together, on a sofa. He'd finished the wine, and poured himself a large brandy, and a smaller one for her. She took a sip, then another. The taste was harsh at first, then hot and pungent, like the after-taste of peppermint. She tried to go on listening, but seemed to have lost the thread. The note of pathos that she'd felt from the start had deepened into sadness; almost tragedy. "You know - when I was a small boy I used to be taken to the cinema, and I enjoyed it so much, I'd beg to be allowed to stay on and see the film round again. And now ... oh God, I've seen the whole show round, time after time. I've had enough. But they won't let me go ... "She felt a lump in her throat, took another sip, seemed to drift for a moment. When next she managed to pay attention, he'd somehow switched to talking about *her*. No, not her exactly, but girls in general; and now the melancholy was somehow combined with a note of accusation. "There you are, all of you, so *young*, with all that vast *energy*, and *enthusiasm*, years and years of it ahead of you, and all looking for some poor devil to spend it on. God forbid ..." Then a sigh, almost a groan. God again. And how had all that about girls got into the monologue? He was holding both her hands in his free hand, tipping the brandy bottle again. She made a vast effort, blinked, tried to get back to looking wide awake and intelligent. Meeting her troubled gaze, he laughed suddenly, put down his glass, gently took away his hand; became brisk and friendly.

"So now, you dear little creature, it's time I sent you home. Isn't it? Where did you say you live?"

And that was that. Soon she was in a taxi, but not alarmed about the vast fare, because he'd paid the driver already. She sat back in a sleepy haze, watching the lighted streets slide past.

But then she sat up straight, jolted out of her trance by amazement. They had swerved into a darker road, drawing up to let other traffic pass. She thought she saw trees, railings ... and a flock of sheep in a wide pasture. In that pause she actually smelt their warm woolly smell, and the scent of grass, and heard the sound of munching. Then the taxi moved on; they were back again in bright suburban streets. Whatever it might have been ... vision, mirage, drunken illusion ... meadow, trees and sheep had vanished completely. And the whole evening, in retrospect, took on the same air of fantasy.

Only, she decided, we were right to call him Lear. She was left with a sense of heartbreak, loneliness and courage: *He weeps by the side of the ocean, He weeps on the top of the hill* - and then gets on with whatever needs doing. All alone in that dusty flat.

How easy, one could see - and, yes, how tempting - to be seduced by so much sadness. But ... he'd more or less warned her off. Though he needn't, she decided, falling asleep. I shan't give him another thought.

16.

Trying to put Arran Green and his pathos out of her mind, she found her thoughts returning next day to that curious glimpse from the taxi - a flock of sheep, a country meadow, enclosed by busy streets. Surely she couldn't have imagined that? It had seemed so real, with sounds and smells to match.

She was still musing about it when they left work in the evening. Sarah went off with Kim Spring. Rowan, about to change into a Highgate train at Camden Town, changed her mind instead and stayed where she was; jumping off six stations later at Hendon.

She didn't really expect to find the meadow again; and at first it seemed that she wasn't going to. The evening had turned grey and thundery, with a storm in the offing. She wished she'd had the sense to go home. Still, as she was here, she might as well search about for a bit.

Wandering at random she found only noisy streets, quieter residential roads. Then she turned a corner; and suddenly there it was ... the high fence lined with chestnut trees, enclosing a field. Sheep standing together, cropping the grass or dotted about like whitish boulders. Familiar smells of late summer, parched turf, bruised yarrow and plantains. Not a mirage after all: a memento of the past. She looked at the scene with deep pleasure.

The first raindrops pattered down, and she moved under the trees. The nearest sheep lifted their heads to watch her with that offended air of theirs, poised for retreat, then began eating again: *Sheep may crossly graze* ... A green shuck dropped and hit her on the head (a surprisingly sharp blow: like the acorn in that folk tale, *Chicken Licken*). As she turned to hurry back to the tube, the skies began to fall, with thunder and lightning and pelting rain. Missing the way, she came to a bus garage and took shelter inside.

Rows of buses stood empty, lighted and waiting. She found one with a sign that said Highgate; but it was locked. A conductor, a black man, appeared and said apologetically,

"Can't wait in here, you know. Not allowed."

"But that's my bus. Couldn't you let me -"

"Due out in twenty minutes. Sorry. No passengers in here."

He nodded towards the bus-stop outside. The rain swirled and hissed; she'd be soaked. Better to run - the tube must be quite near. She was moving away when he called,

"No, don't go, please. Come with me. I'll show you a place to wait."

Following, she found herself at the foot of a narrow stair, leading upwards into darkness.

Sheer folly, to go up there with him: the sort of thing one was always warned about. Yet something in his face made refusal impossible: a patient look, resigned to her distrust, half amused, yet rueful; knowing quite well that, if he'd been white, an ordinary London bus conductor, she probably wouldn't have hesitated. She followed him up the stair.

He opened a door at the top; and she stepped into a scene of bright lights and chat, clinking cups, tobacco haze. A staff room. He smiled slightly at her look of relief, drew up a chair, fetched her a cup of coffee and went off to the snooker table; returning presently to say that her bus would be leaving. As she began to thank him, he laughed, leaned down and said softly in her ear,

"You see ... we're not all black savages."

This summer the streets were full of such newcomers. After that, she became more aware of them. Barristers with dark faces, set off by silvery wigs and snow-white bands, were of course no novelty in the courts. She heard one, a popular and ebullient Nigerian, telling a pair of grinning prison officers, "Come along, you white trash, take me down to my client." But then it was startling when a visiting South African banged out of the press box as Devi came in.

Perhaps the varying attitudes they found - indifference, hostility, tolerance, patronage - drove some of them to demonstration or to private jokes. A reporter from Ceylon had his own brand of leg-pulling. From a fictional Indian schoolboy, discovered at his prep school, he'd borrowed a trick of quiet malapropisms and would drop them casually into a conversation: 'just a flash in the park', 'still green behind the ears', 'like Potiphar's wife, above suspicion'. Few people ever noticed; sometimes, if they did, they would kindly put him right. This, Rowan guessed, was a high point in the game.

One evening she was in a public library, checking through newspaper files for Alex, when a West Indian youth walked in, strolled to the far end of the room, turned and announced dramatically,

"I am here to tell you that I am Jesus Christ, returned to earth for a new ministry."

He paused and looked about him.

At once a hush descended. The place became like the Sleeping Beauty's court. All sounds died away. Readers at the tables, browsers at the shelves, librarians behind the counter, all froze in horrified embarrassment, united in their resolve to ignore him. He repeated his announcement with variations, and plunged into a rambling sermon. No one coughed or rustled. No face was raised, let alone a voice. Nothing disturbed the chill of total repudiation.

Several minutes dragged by. At length he stopped speaking, raised his arms in blessing, bowed and walked out with dignity. Slowly, avoiding one another's eyes, people came out of their trance and went on with their occupations.

Rowan had a glimpse of his face as he sauntered pass the glass wall. Like the bus conductor, he was smiling faintly to himself.

17

To dismiss Arran Green from her mind wasn't possible, she found. He now appeared in court more often, and would take her out for a lunchtime drink if she could get away. Sometimes too she was invited to dinner in some restaurant, and fed on dishes new to her - grouse, red mullet like grilled goldfish, crêpes Suzette, zabaglione - while he discoursed fluently on any topic that took his fancy. Once, at a table near by, she recognised a popular actor who, with his wife and little daughters, attracted curious or admiring notice from other diners. She saw that Arran too was observing them discreetly, and waiting to see if he would make any comment. This, when it came, was unexpected. Looking after the party as they left, he said with dispassionate interest -

"Family life! Extraordinary. It must be like keeping white rabbits. Very pretty. And amusing ... if you like rabbits. Even a solace, perhaps, sometimes. But - a total *blank* on any other level. Quite mindless so far as the man's concerned. And he's stuck with all of them for years."

She stared at him, then down at her plate. As usual, her thoughts flew to Ralph. Could he ever feel like Arran? - or that man in the tea-room the other day, so bitter about marriage? Wasn't theirs just a cynical elderly reaction - *nothing to do with us*?

One day, of course, if they escaped the Bomb, she and Ralph would be older too; but somehow one couldn't believe that would change anything. In childhood, when a month seemed as long as a year, one had taken it for granted that people stayed the same age all the time. She remembered thinking, I'm glad they made me *young*. Illogically, in a way she still felt this. *And we'd never be like them, we'd be different ...*

Then, looking up, she realised that Arran was watching her intently; sensing her protest, and wondering about it. He now began for the first time to draw her out, encouraging her for the rest of the evening to talk about herself. And again his verdict was unexpected.

"This is really no life for you. Is it?"

She was too astonished to reply at once. He persisted,

"I think you should be in the country, with all those horses and dogs and bogs you've been pining for."

A strange notion; and totally mistaken ... True, she'd once meant to work with horses, to live in the woods somewhere. But that idea, like other childish things, had been eclipsed. (In New Zealand, perhaps, it might be revived? Safer not to pursue such visions. Well - not yet.)

But a day or two later she was reminded of Arran Green's remark. She and Mike were leaving Belsize Park station, on their way to a local court, when a riderless horse came careering down the pavement, swerving dangerously among the passers-by. As it reached them, a car sped out of a side turning. The horse reared up in its path, plunged and almost fell to its knees as the driver stopped just in time. At the same moment, Mike and Rowan had each put out a hand, catching the bridle on either side. The terrified horse recovered itself and stood between them, sweating and shuddering; they patted and spoke to it reassuringly. But then, as curious onlookers gathered round, Mike groaned,

"What the heck do we do with it?"

"Police station?"

They hesitated, and thought of leading the fractious creature up the hill, and up a steep flight of steps, to a far from cordial welcome by Hampstead police. But they were spared. A young trooper, red-faced and furious, came pelting on the scene, snatched the bridle from them and led his mount away, back to the Heath.

Afterwards, laughing, they asked one another - "What on earth possessed us?" But they knew that they'd acted instinctively: one couldn't help trying to protect a frightened horse. Years of learning to look after animals must have left their mark.

As the summer advanced, the girls had found their lives changing; they no longer spent the evenings together. Sarah would disappear after work with a murmured excuse, or none, rarely coming home before midnight. Rowan guessed that she was having a serious affair, but had no idea with whom, and no intention of asking. Caro too had taken to staying out late. Left to enjoy the garden alone, Rowan would feed the hedgehogs at twilight, taking extra saucers of milk for the young ones, who were now driven off by their mothers with fierce 'tissing' noises. Also she began to buy tinned food for hungry cats that waited in the shadows, gaunt and avid, roaming loose while their owners were on holiday. A spotted flycatcher sat out of reach on the handle of the garden roller, alert for midges; the faint *snip-snip* of its little beak went on until darkness fell.

Sarah was reticent about her lover, but would sometimes pretend to speculate about Arran Green and his intentions.

"Be careful. He may think you'd make a nice docile child-wife."

"At our age! No, he just likes someone to talk to."

"Oh, *talk* ... what about?"

"Wars. Armies. Greeks and Romans. 'History, philosophy and kindred subjects.'"

"Fascinating."

"Well, he is, rather."

Sarah asked suddenly in a teasing undertone - "And when will you see *him* again?"

"*Him!* Who?"

51

"That man you're in love with. Whoever he is."

"I'm not - "And then she admitted, "Oh. One day perhaps. Not yet."

"In Ireland, is he?"

"Sometimes."

Could Sarah possibly have hit on the truth? But no more was said. And next year, when she left for New Zealand, she'd simply let people think she was visiting Lizzie and Rufus. Meanwhile, at work, there were these casual amusing friendships: with Arran Green, Mike, Toby, Devi - engaged no doubt to some ravishing beauty in Srinagar - and Derry Gillespie, who of course must be far too old for anything else.

She and Sarah were each to have a week's holiday in the autumn, and Mother had begun to refer to this in her letters, assuming that Rowan would come to Nine Wells. But Rowan felt it was too soon to meet her family again. She needed more time to grow into her new adult self and to build up her confidence.

Grandmother, she knew, thought her far too young for so much freedom; but this was natural, from one of her generation. Grandfather doubtless thought the same, but could be trusted nowadays to keep his views to himself. No need to take their disapproval seriously. It was the parents who, from real concern perhaps (one must try to be fair) would be sure to undermine her, disparaging her looks and ideas and any adventures she was rash enough to admit to.

So, when the time came, she must find an excuse for not going. Christmas would be quite soon enough.

18.

The brilliant summer weather held on into September. Then came a showery interval. At Sessions, a good-natured caretaker, inviting Mike and Rowan up to the roof to see a kestrel perched on a building near by, appeared like a coastguard in streaming oilskins and sou'-wester, field-glasses slung round his neck. In a high corridor, raindrops blew in from the roof door, affronting the court cat as it inspected a row of savoury dishes put down for its evening meal.

Alone in the house at Highgate, Rowan checked the television news for Caro (nothing from Cyprus) then ate her cold supper quickly and went out into the rain.

Robins, thrushes, a travelling chiffchaff, even a late blackbird were singing for pleasure at this break in the drought. Summer flowers, their scent and colour freshened, mingled with freak spring blossoms, wallflower and polyanthus. Next door, the Pringles' laburnum had flowered again, hanging a few bright tassels and green pods over the fence. Their garden was quiet, free from the sounds of Robin and Linnet and their friends; they must still be away at their country cottage.

Crossing the high Archway on her way to the park, seeing the dome of St. Joseph's in a gleam of watery light, she had a swift pang of recollection: her first morning in Florence, her first afternoon in Oxford - both magical. On a wall beside Highgate Hill she found a plaque inscribed to some poet, Andrew Marvell, and a fragment of verse drifted across her mind, just out of reach, something about *Time's winged chariot,* from one of those poems where the lover was trying to get his girl friend into bed, so it didn't appear in old school books ... What a year this had been! And, yes, the time had flown, day after crowded day.

Next morning the sun was shining, the temperature soaring again. Yesterday the black cat had strolled about the court corridors, enjoying the cooler air, snubbing anyone who tried to stroke it for luck. Today it had returned to summer torpor. A snob of the first water, it usually chose to sleep in the chairman's private room. Finding the door shut, it sulked for a while outside, then strolled into court and jumped into his chair on the Bench. Here, curled on a black velvet cushion, it was so well camouflaged that Judge Huff's usher could affect not to notice it. He flickered one eyelid towards Sarah and Rowan as the Judge came in. To their disappointment, Judge Huff saw the cat just in time before taking his seat, glared round for help, failed to catch the usher's eye, then dislodged the creature himself, to their mutual displeasure.

It was this larky usher, ever resourceful, who rescued Sarah half-way through the morning, when she came close to fainting from the heat, and led her away to be revived with brandy in the judges' dining-room.

Surprisingly, for one of her resilience, she had seemed to wilt as the burning weeks went on, and was now glad to be sent on leave.

She went off to recover at a bachelor cousin's house in Norfolk, rejoicing because she would miss an event they had all three rather dreaded: a dinner party next door with the Pringles. Thinking they knew by now the kind of food to expect, they were not surprised to hear that Mr. Pringle himself had urgent business in the north and would not be home in time to act as host: his place would be taken by Beth's nephew, Gilbert, a medical student who had come to lodge with them.

Beth, new to country pursuits and full of enthusiasm, would bring back green walnuts, blackberries, sloes and other gleanings from their cottage weekends. Sarah, waiting for her taxi, predicted with relish, "Nut cutlets. Blackberry wine. Dandelion salad. Oh, and beards and sandals -"

After this, it was almost disappointing to find quite ordinary drinks on offer, and a normal-looking crowd, conventionally dressed. But their hostess made up for this. Wearing one of her flowing Pre-Raphaelite gowns, dark green and terracotta, with gold earrings, her beautiful chestnut hair plaited and wound about her head, Beth looked happy and excited as a child. The children themselves, appearing in pyjamas, were on their best behaviour, quiet and demure. They'd been so useful, their mother said, helping in the kitchen. Soon, bribed with raspberry syrup and potato crisps, they retired upstairs.

They left behind a white rat, which scampered about in terror, chattering at anyone who tried to catch it. One guest, genuinely afraid of rats and mice, had to be calmed and reassured. For the rest, however, it passed as a whimsical prank. Robin, protesting innocence, collected his pet, and they sat down to dinner.

Gilbert, the medical student, poured red wine, and Beth served out quiches, smoking hot, filled with bacon, cheese and mushrooms, and freshly garnished with chopped herbs and tiny green peas.

"All our own herbs and vegetables," she said proudly, "Wild garlic ... oh, and wild mushrooms too. The children picked them, I do hope they're all right!"

She laughed. The guests smiled politely. Gilbert came back from the kitchen with another bottle.

Rowan felt a cold shudder down her spine. She stared at Beth, speechless. A voice in her head had begun to warn her - Stop them. You'll have to stop them. They don't understand. Beth doesn't understand.

Aunt Lizard's voice.

From far away in the past Lizzie had recalled a grim experience. Staying somewhere in the country; going to morning service at the village church, where a troop of little schoolgirls appeared with their teachers. City children, camping in a farmer's field; having the time of their lives, someone had said. But by the next Sunday several were in hospital, desperately ill, and one was dead.

The delights of camping had included picking mushrooms for breakfast. But they didn't know, and neither did their elders, how to tell a mushroom from a Death Cap. At the inquest, the farmer wept and said he only knew one way to tell for certain - "take along someone brought up in the country."

So what about the Pringles? How would they know? And what about these quiches, full of dark mushroom slivers?

In a moment, she thought, they'll start eating. But I can't let them, I must speak up ... and wreck Beth's party.

Does it have to be me? Surely someone else must have realised the danger? They'd all heard what Beth said. She glanced frantically round the table.

No one looked in the least perturbed. Luckily, they hadn't yet begun to eat. On Gilbert's prompting, they were drinking to their absent host.

Gilbert: he was a medical student - surely *he* would have heard of mushroom victims? Why hadn't he said anything? Then she realised - when Beth said that, he was out of the room, out of earshot. So it has to be me ...

"Gilbert!"

Her voice came out as a croak, too low to attract attention. She spoke again, on a high frightened note, "Gilbert! Listen!"

They heard that. They all stopped talking and turned to look at her. She stammered,

"Beth. You said - the children picked the mushrooms - down at the cottage? And - you *hoped* they're all right?"

Beth was still smiling. "The mushrooms! Why yes ... but of course they're all right. What is it, Rowan? What's the matter?"

"But, you see ... they might be all wrong. I mean it, Beth ..." She turned to Gilbert, willing him with all her strength to understand.

He put down the bottle he was holding. He stared at her, and she saw his face change, surprise giving way to doubt, then to startled realisation.

"God, she's right. Hold on, everyone. Beth darling, I hate to tell you, but ..."

The evening, after all, was saved from disaster. Beth rallied bravely. She opened a box packed ready for the cottage: emergency supplies, great tins of spaghetti, mince, tomato purée, and heated the contents briskly. There were also tins of mushrooms, but somehow no one felt inclined to open these. The guests rushed about, wielding tin openers, clearing the table, finding fresh plates, keeping up Beth's spirits with a flow of jokes and laughter.

Gilbert's contribution was to dig out a textbook and read aloud extracts on mushroom poisoning.

"About 90% of deaths attributable to *Amanita phalloides,* the Death Cap ... The toxin is not destroyed by cooking. Symptoms do not occur until eight to twenty-four hours after ingestion, by which time much of the toxin has been absorbed into the body ... Death occurs after two to ten days of great suffering. A single cap of *Amanita phalloides* in a fungus dish is more than sufficient to cause death."

Clearly he felt driven to justify his veto. And, after this recital, no one was inclined to blame him. But Rowan still felt guilty. She had started the panic, quite needlessly perhaps. The mushrooms were probably as innocent as the jacket potatoes. Indeed Beth, with gentle obstinacy, continued to say as much, though she was too kind to let this seem a direct reproach.

And Rowan continued to wonder; until, one evening later in the week, Gilbert called to see her and Caro.

He'd had the quiches analysed. There was nothing wrong with the mushrooms. They'd been quite OK.

Rowan nodded glumly. Just as she'd feared. Caro began, "Still - you couldn't risk it -"

"Wait. Let me tell you."

He'd got hold of Robin and Linnet, he said, when their parents were out of the way, shaken the truth from the little brutes and given them the fright of their lives.

They admitted that they hadn't gone mushrooming at all. Too boring. They'd 'borrowed' some money - "out of Beth's handbag, if I know those two" - and bought mushrooms from the village shop, and spent the afternoon at a cinema.

"So Beth was right. *Agaricus campestris.* Common field mushrooms. Not a Death Cap in sight. But ... thank God you spoke up, Rowan. Those quiches were lethal. Chock full of poison."

"No!"

"Oh yes. What a party that would have been. People throwing up right and left, passing out ... 999, ambulances ... " He grinned, enjoying their stupefaction.

"But - if the mushrooms were all right ... What was it? Who did it? *Gilbert!* You can't mean - those children?"

"Can't I?" He mimicked, "'We didn't mean any harm - they were just like little peas' ..."

"But *what* -?"

"Just another of their charming little games. Remember those green peas - scattered all over the quiches? Know what they were really? Laburnum seeds. Off the tree in the garden."

19.

Writing to Aunt Lizard that night, meaning to pour out the tale of the mushroom dinner party, Rowan found herself instead describing something different. As she left Bow Street court that afternoon, heading for the tube, she passed a little shop never noticed before; a dim cave, open to the street, filled with florists' greenery - bales of moss, tubs of beech boughs and evergreens, freshly sprayed. Their scent was suddenly overwhelming.

For a moment she was back in the wilderness at Nine Wells, where as a small child, sent away from wartime England, she had spent happy hours alone. Again, as on that day by Ullswater, the thought darted across her mind - why I am here, what am I doing in London? When Arran Green had accused her of pining she had denied it eagerly after her first surprise. Yet now, breathing that aromatic blend, leaf and needles, sap and resin, she felt an aching sense of loss, and was almost ready to throw up her job and start life again; on some hick newspaper perhaps, where she could live among trees and fields and horses, and still save up for New Zealand.

This flight of fancy lasted through a stifling rush-hour journey, then faded rapidly. At home she looked down from her attic window into the treetops and felt as usual that she had the best of both worlds.

One couldn't speak of this to anyone but Lizzie, but *she* was always safe. Probably she felt homesick herself at times, exiled down there with the tree-ferns and the English oak trees.

As she finished her letter, dusk was creeping over the garden. She switched off the light and listened for the first owl-call.

The pair were now hunting singly, perhaps guarding a late nest in the wood; but one need not fear for their safety as one had feared for the blackcaps and flycatchers. No cat or rat or magpie would challenge those beaks and talons; and the earlier darkness would protect them from human intrusion. Of all the thousands living round about, few were even likely to notice the dark winged shadows floating above the street lamps. Night time was another, safer world.

Except for one night in the year. But of this neither she nor the owls had any premonition.

20

With the first chill of October, change was in the air. Devi was going to Reuters, Mike to a provincial evening paper; Toby had been called up for national service. New people would be coming. Meanwhile - Rowan explained in a letter to Nine Wells - her holiday had better be postponed.

Breck, they now heard, had had a brief spell of leave in Athens, but at too short notice for Caro to join him. Whatever she felt about this, she kept it to herself. Sarah too was quiet and preoccupied since her return from Norfolk; as though not yet recovered from her fit of lassitude, she was content just now to spend her free time idling at home. It seemed that her love affair must be broken off; but amicably, Rowan thought, as she appeared quite happy.

Rowan herself passed a more festive month. Arran Green began taking her to the opera, and she came to know Bow Street by night, lights glowing from the great pillared house opposite the darkened court; and, as they left, the flower market stirring into life near by. But this pleasant interlude was short.

For these occasions, surprisingly, he had sent her a charming dress, with a black velvet top, low-cut, long-sleeved, and glossy bell-shaped skirt striped in black and white: dismissing her thanks with -

"A birthday present, if you like. I dare say you have a birthday some time?"

"Yes! November the fifth."

A goodbye present too, it proved: by then he would have left for Scotland, where he had some property, to spend the rest of the year.

"And you? Still knocking about in London?"

"Well. I'll be going to Ireland, just for Christmas."

"H'm. Remember what I told you."

And, a week after his departure, she did remember.

There was a letter for her one morning. A stiff brown envelope, with typed address; a lawyer's letter, it proved, polite, formal and mysterious. She was asked to call on Saturday November the fifth at an office in Lincoln's Inn; and the writer was hers faithfully, B. Handyside, of Handyside & Glover, Solicitors.

She made an early morning appointment; and found further mystery. Mr. Handyside, a bird-like individual, sharp-eyed and sharp-featured, received her with more formal politeness, and explained that he was instructed to hand her *this*: another stiff brown envelope, unsealed, and in it a door key. Not a latch key, but larger and heavier. The key to a furnished cottage in Cornwall, whose address she would also find in the envelope.

She drew out a paper and read: The Orchard House, Sheepskin, St. Max, near Farmouth.

The property, said Mr. Handyside, was unoccupied at present, and their client wished to make it over to her, rent free, for an indefinite period; in fact, for as long as she might wish to make use of it.

She looked at him in blank amazement. Their client? A cottage in Cornwall?

"I don't understand - I don't know anyone there! Are you quite sure it's me you want?"

Yes, he was quite sure.

"But - *you* must know who -"

Smiling blandly, he called her his dear young lady, and repeated that these were 'our instructions'. He was not at liberty to give their client's name; was indeed forbidden to do so. To more bewildered questions he returned the same bland and courteous stonewalling response, as though impersonating some old-world lawyer.

Then, seeing her at a loss, he became reassuring. He could promise her, and-another faint smile - her guardians, that the offer was perfectly genuine, and their client known to the firm for many years: a person of utmost probity, who simply preferred to remain anonymous, to act in her interests, and make her a gift that, it was hoped, would give her pleasure and also prove beneficial.

Beneficial ... suddenly light dawned. Arran Green, and his advice - that she ought to be living in the country! He must be this nameless benefactor? And how like him to give it in this safe secretive way, without involving himself directly!

Not, of course, that she could possibly accept his offer.

She told inscrutable Mr.Handyside, "I believe I know who. Would you - will you thank him for me, please? And - and I'll think about it."

He bowed her out and said, becoming for a moment almost human, "Enjoy yourself."

As to that, she thought, I'm enjoying myself already. Arran knows I am. No point in gallivanting off to Cornwall, whatever he thinks. Kind of him though. And I suppose I *might* take a look at the place one day, before I return this key ...

Back in the press room, Alex sprang a surprise of his own.

"Farmouth, eh? That's near Faro. Like to go down there and help send out an inquest?"

"An *inquest*?"

"A big one. Jamie's been on to me." Jamie, his son, was running a news agency in Faro. "He says he'd be glad of a hand. Monday morning. How about it?"

"Oh - and then - I *could* go and see this cottage!"

"Of course you could. Take your holiday, why not? Don't desert us though," he added. "Jamie went down there for a week, and never came back."

21

At home she found birthday letters; a card from Aunt Lizard, a cheque from Nine Wells. When she returned from Cornwall she would buy winter clothes, an A-line coat perhaps, and a huge shaggy sweater like Sarah's latest.

Caro and Sarah were both out. She would meet them at the theatre for her birthday treat, "Salad Days" again. She ate a dripping fried egg sandwich and watched children scuffling for chestnuts under the tree at the front of the house. At dusk she went upstairs: just time to see the owls, before she left.

The birds had changed their evening routine. They no longer set off to hunt as soon as they were awake, but hovered over the wood, with little cries and trills, persuading their young ones to fly. One by one the fledglings were coaxed from the nest and brought out to sit in a row on a straight bough at the top of an old ash tree: five small dark shapes, huddled in their new soft feathers, with a parent on either side. Presently one of the pair would slip away for food, while the other encouraged the young to try their wings in short fluttering excursions.

She had watched them night after night; but this was to be the last.

Just as they settled on their bough, a rocket roared up from a garden near by, bursting over the ash tree in a cascade of green and silver sparks. Another followed, and another. The barrage was taken up in neighbouring gardens, filling the air with fire and smoke, rushing winds and violent explosions. The owls vanished, never to return.

---ooo---

II

Here had lived an elder race, to which we look back with disquietude. The country ... was really a home to it, and the graver sides of life, the deaths, the partings, the yearnings for love, have their deepest expression in the heart of the fields.

E.M. Forster: *Howard's End*

22

"Silence! All manner of persons having business before the coroner draw nigh and give your attendance. And if any person can give evidence for Her Majesty the Queen how, when and by what means the following came to their deaths, let him come forth and he shall be heard ..."

The inquest went on its dreadful way. Once before, when Rowan had been in a coroner's court, the first witness had broken down at the dreaded opening question - *Whose is the body you have just seen?* - then forced himself to go through with the business. Today, more terribly, no bodies remained to be identified. Four small boys had found an old rusty sea-mine washed up on the beach, and tinkered with it secretly week after week. One of them had grown bored in the end, and wandered off, seconds before the mine blew up; and so found himself telling the court how his friends came to their death. Searchers had combed the beach, the cliffs and surrounding countryside, hoping by some miracle to find the boys alive, hurled away by the blast. But they had vanished without trace.

The story was ordered by the London papers, and by Reuters, who would send it all over the world. Rowan spent most of the morning dictating instalments from a telephone box by the town hall. Afterwards she and Jamie typed copies in his office, a little wooden hut beside Faro station from which he ran his agency, Far News. Rowan packed them into a stack of envelopes marked Urgent Copy and handed them over to the guard on the next London train.

She had agreed to cover another inquest down in Farmouth on the following morning. It was now late afternoon. Tired and sad, drained by all she had heard, she no longer felt much interest in finding the cottage at Sheepskin. The alternative - another night in the lodging house where she had slept last night - was not inviting either. She was tempted to forget her promise to Jamie, forget the key in her pocket: simply jump on the waiting train and go home. One grey day in this sombre slate and granite town seemed quite enough.

The guard still paced up and down, green flag under his arm, whistle ready. As she hesitated, there was a shout from the outer office, then a porter and another man rushed on to the platform and began piling long flat boxes into the van. Flowers With Care, she saw in black lettering on the box lids, and an address in Covent Garden.

Covent Garden ... but she'd just come from there. Rather stupid to go straight back ... wasn't it?

The doors slammed, the whistle shrieked. She stood still, watching the train slide away.

But when she asked about trains to St. Max, the porter shook his head: nothing till evening. Then he yelled after the man who had brought the boxes -

"Peter! Hold on!"

He turned in enquiry.

"Young lady going your way!"

As he came slowly back, she saw that he was young, blond, tanned, with bright hair curling about his ears. She also saw that he felt much as she did herself, too fagged to be inclined for company. He asked curtly, "Where is it you want?"

"Doesn't matter, thanks - I'll find a taxi -"

He sighed and waited.

"Well, St. Max station, I was told -"

He jerked his head, inviting her to follow. Outside he opened the door of a van, muddy and battered looking, with a painted sign: Peter Thoransen, Woods Farm, St. Max. Inside it smelled agreeably of straw and crushed violet leaves. They rattled out of the town into a countryside of rushy fields, iron gates, stone hedges. Like Ireland, she thought, but with dark blue moorland instead of mountains in the distance.

Suddenly he braked sharply.

Some way off, a man was standing in the road and waving frantically. As they came near he shouted, "Stop, stop, help -" and pointed to the roadside, where a car was slewed across the grass. The van drew alongside, and they saw a woman crouching in the front seat, her head down, as though she had fainted. The man dashed forward, crying, "My wife - a baby - car broke down - quick, can you get us to hospital?"

Between them the two men helped her into the back of the van, where she lay with closed eyes, propped against her husband's knees. Rowan thought they would turn back to the town; but they sped onward, faster and faster. The woman began to writhe and gasp, and the man held her, cursing under his breath -

"My fault - should have started hours ago -"

She seemed to recover after a minute. The gasping stopped, and she whispered - "No, my fault. Thought I'd wait - this time - skip the castor oil bit -" She tried to laugh, drew breath sharply and seemed to go into a convulsion, giving short harsh cries that changed to moans, then to strenuous rhythmic gasping. Rowan looked in terror at Peter Thoransen, who had been driving with set white face, gazing straight ahead. Now he slowed and looked back, stammering -

"Is it - is she - *Shall I stop?*"

"No, no, no - get on - for God's sake, hurry!"

They shot forward again, the van rocking and shuddering. Now they were passing a long stone wall beside a tree scattered park. The van swerved aside on to a gravel sweep where high iron gates stood open; passed

68

a little ornate lodge, slowed to bump over a cattle grid, then raced uphill under an avenue of yellow lime trees. Ahead, behind dark hedges, Rowan saw a great grey house with rows of tall windows. They rounded a bend and came to a stone-pillared entrance.

A motor coach stood there, its engine running. Nurses in blue cloaks were getting in, smoking, laughing and chatting in off-duty mood. No one glanced their way.

The van driver pulled up, sounded his horn, flung himself out and raced to the front door, calling for help, while Rowan and the husband tried to lift the woman to her feet. A nurse came out of the house at a leisurely pace, as though to rebuke any fuss and panic; but after one glance she changed her mind and acted at high speed. The patient was whisked into the house and out of sight, her husband looking back for a moment to croak something heartfelt and inaudible, before he too disappeared.

The coach had driven away. They looked at one another, speechless with relief, too shaken to smile. Then he said, a shade more amiably than before,

"Well then. St. Max station, wasn't it? Then where?"

"Oh - a place called Sheepskin -"

"Sheskin? So here you are." He waved a hand. "Sheepskin House."

"No, I ... is this a nursing-home then?"

"City hospital. Maternity wing."

"Yes, well ... I want somewhere else, I think. The orchard house."

"Do you!" He looked sceptical. "You sure? No one living *there* now."

"I know." She produced the key. He said dubiously,

"H'm. Look. You can go that way -" pointing to a gate in a wall. "Through the gardens. You'll see a door at the other end. Then down to the river -"

"Oh! a *river*?"

"The river Far."

Interest suddenly revived. She broke in, "Yes, yes ... *thanks*. And for the lift -" and moved away. He called after her,

"Wait a minute. How will you get back?"

She checked and looked round impatiently.

"No bus tonight. No train till late. The inn's shut."

"But I'm going to stay there!"

He moved nearer, saying carefully, as though to a child,

"You do realise ... ? It's been empty for months. Dark soon. It's a lonely place ..."

She stared at him, thinking - *but it won't be like that*!

A secret picture had taken shape in her mind: a place of light and warmth, ready and waiting for her - as though she were really a child again, travelling with Aunt Lizard. Little thin tan Lizard ... slipping into yet another snug crevice, unerringly chosen, carefully prepared, even at a distance ...

But Lizzie was thousands of miles away, with another child. This arrival was bound to be different.

She felt the chill of disenchantment, and said coldly,

"I'll be all right."

At least he might let her find out her own mistakes ... but he added, with the same note of concern,

"Sure?" And then, before she could move - "Got a torch?"

Seeing by her look that she hadn't, he shrugged, smiled faintly, reached into the van and put a heavy flashlight into her hand.

Then he was gone. The van backed, swung round and sped downhill into the avenue. She was left alone with her misgivings.

23

The narrow wrought-iron gate led into a walled garden, with straight neat gravel paths and rows of espalier fruit trees. A melancholy autumn garden, smelling of musty box hedges, fig trees, the bitter tang of chrysanthemums and celery. On the far side she went through a green wooden door into a wilderness of rough grass and shrubberies, high dark conifers, copper beeches still bright with leaves. A fresh wave of scents - fir, laurel, cedars, beech leaves, wet moss - seemed somehow familiar, and suddenly she realised - this was the smell of the shop in Bow Street, many times intensified. Excitement stirred again, and she hurried on.

Stone figures loomed here and there in the shadows; a beautiful youth, Antinous perhaps, a faun, a nymph or goddess; lions prancing on either side of a mossy marble seat. Further on, the ground dipped sharply, and she saw the river, a thread of silver in a rocky bed, spanned by a narrow stone footbridge. Now she could smell mist, rushes, rotting water plants. Just above the bridge stood a little domed tower, like a folly, and beside it a rowan tree with tawny berries catching the last sunlight.

A robin flitted out of its branches, darted across the river and was lost in a tangle of ancient apple trees. Her eyes followed the speck of scarlet until it disappeared. And then, beyond the little orchard, she saw a grey cottage.

Stepping on to the bridge, she leaned on the parapet and looked up at the orchard house. Light from the west flashed in an upper window, as though someone in there had lit a candle. Then, as she watched, the gleam faded and died. Inside, the dark waited.

And her heart sank. That wretched man, Peter something ... of course he'd been right. She should have come here in the morning, with hours of daylight ahead; not at sunset on a dreary November evening. One couldn't spend the night in a cold dark house, with no lights, no food, no fire. She'd forgotten how soon it would be nightfall.

"Idiot," she told herself. It seemed so obvious now. And he'd said the inn was shut. No bus or train. So what next?

Find her way back to that lodge, perhaps. They might have a telephone; she could ring for a taxi. If not she'd have to walk, stay in the town again, and come back tomorrow with proper supplies. After all, she was in no hurry, she was on holiday - except for that second inquest tomorrow morning. This had been a false start, but next time she'd do better.

Still ... now she *was* here she might just take a look inside the house? The sun had disappeared, dusk was falling rapidly; but at least, thanks to *him*, she had a torch.

She left the bridge and scrambled up the grassy slope that ran down beside the orchard. At the side of the house a short flight of steps led up to the entrance. The key turned, she lifted a latch, and the heavy door creaked open. She stepped cautiously inside, keeping one hand on the latch, and beamed the light about.

She was in a long high room, like a little barn, with a stone-flagged floor. The window on her left was a shadowy mirror. Taking another step, she saw her reflection, pale and wide-eyed, ready to dart back at the first hint of anything unwelcome.

And suddenly the reflection laughed at her. There was nothing here to be wary of, let alone afraid. The place felt warm and friendly, a refuge, like someone's home. *My* home for tonight, she decided: and shut the door, and threw down her pack.

On her right, set in the end wall, there was an open fireplace, with a fire laid ready, and a kettle on a hook. In growing surprise she saw logs and kindling stacked by the hearth; a crock of water; sheepskin mats on the floor, and a long couch with rugs and cushions; a table with candles and matches in china holders, like bedroom candles at Nine Wells. She lit three, clicked off the torch and stood watching the tiny flames as they swayed, reared up and settled into a tremulous glow.

In the war, there had been no electric lights in Grandfather's house; only oil lamps and candles, and sometimes only firelight, because of wartime shortages: moonlight or starlight to go to bed by. The sense of homecoming deepened.

Beside the candles she saw a tray with tea-things, a little green tea-caddy, a biscuit box, a bowl of eggs, another of apples and hazel-nuts. *Just as though she were expected.* As though someone had come here to get the place ready for her. As though Lizzie had really been in charge after all.

Then it dawned on her - of course she *was* expected! That lawyer had assumed she'd be coming, he must have arranged it all. And someone would have told him to. Arran Green - if he *were* the owner? This forethought would be typical of him. She'd heard him say, in one of those irascible throwaway speeches - "Oh, *women*, you have to feed them and fuss over them and butter them up, such a bore." And she'd laughed, never connecting any of that with herself, or herself with those imperious demanding women in his life. But - she saw now - he'd really treated her in just the same way. And he knew how to organise; and how to live in comfort. It seemed that, once again, she was reaping the benefit.

The sticks were dry, the fire lit amiably. She sat on the rug, feeding it with twigs and cones until the logs burned steadily under the hanging kettle.

At this end of the room, table, couch and fireplace formed a sheltered den. She stood up and switched on the torch again, and shone it down to the far end. Shadows leaped and hovered over whitewashed walls, dark rafters, doors. Time enough to inspect all that after tea.

Sitting close to the fire, she heard the low grumbling of the kettle; then another sound, intermittent at first, becoming softly persistent. She'd

72

heard that before, beside the kitchen stove at Nine Wells. Cheered by the spreading warmth, a cricket had awakened and begun to chirp from some cranny in the hearth-stones.

The kettle stopped muttering, gave a lurch and started to hum, then to sing. She made tea and sat on the couch to drink it, slipping two eggs into the bubbling water.

Grandmother had a tea-caddy like this: a small shiny green box with white butterflies on it ... one of thousands, someone had told her, brought over long ago in the old tea-clippers. Her teacup was familiar too; pale blue and white, with a picture of a church, and tiny lettering that said Stratford-on-Avon. Now that *was* odd! She'd seen cups like this in the Nine Wells china-cupboard, faint blue and pink and green, with different pictures, Haddon Hall, Fountains Abbey, a hunting scene ... but nothing seemed really odd by now. Perhaps they too had been made in thousands, like the tea-caddies, like willow-pattern china ... perhaps she was growing too drowsy to take things in properly, let alone feel surprised. She roused herself to scoop out the eggs from the kettle, hard-boiled by now, and ate them with biscuits, gazing out into the darkness.

She could hear the low ripple of water on stones, the soft plash of a waterfall, and catch glimpses of pale waving foliage - pampas grasses, high reeds - and swirling mist. Once she thought some creature - a stray dog? - bumped against the door and made a grunting, snuffling sound. Once, too, she fancied that a face appeared for a second at the window: a child's face, impish, owlish (spectacled?) Could she have imagined that? Nothing there now.

She yawned, suddenly as drowsy as though it were midnight instead of early evening. Last night, in that bed-and-breakfast house at Faro, she'd been too tired to sleep soundly. It had seemed long years since her early trek to Highgate tube, through drifts of dead leaves, with spent firework husks crunching underfoot, and the acrid smells of gunpowder and cold bonfires hanging in the air. (*Remember, remember* ... but the lost owls were best forgotten, memory was far too painful.) The quick walk in frosty starlight had brought a welcome sense of escape that persisted on the journey west, past brown ploughlands, parched meadows, banks thick with rusty autumn weeds; in and out of red cliffs, with flashing glimpses of the sea; along the estuary and up the river, with its flocks of wintering birds; then across the bridge into this county of deep woods and little grey deserted stations.

Today's inquest had quenched that carefree feeling for a time; but here she felt it waiting again, somewhere beyond night and sleep, outside the ring of candlelight.

The fire flickered, the cricket chirped, the candle flames swayed as a thin cold draught swept down the room. She thought the flames made a tiny

73

sound like the flitter of a moth on a window-pane. She shut her eyes to listen.

The candle flames went on shining behind her eyelids; now she thought they sounded like people whispering. People *waiting* ... and she seemed to know what for. She remembered the woman they'd brought to Sheepskin House ... but that was ages ago, her baby *must* be here by now? Or was this a dream? She held her breath, waiting with those other shadowy watchers for the first cry of the new-born.

Before it came she fell into a deeper sleep that lasted without dreams, while the fire died into ashes and the candle flames sank down among loops of melting tallow that people in Ireland had called shrouds.

24

When she opened her eyes, dim light filled the room.   Daylight.
But, looking out, there was nothing to see but clouds of white mist, and the
tips of the higher trees on the far bank.   Down there out of sight the river
murmured.   Then, opening the door, she heard the far-off roar of the sea.

Oh, the sea ... I'll go there *first*, she thought.

But indoors again she hesitated, seeing last night's tea dregs and
eggshells; and went reluctantly in search of a kitchen.   At the end of the
room she found two doors.   One led into a stone-flagged cell, ice-cold, with
slate shelves, stone sink, a pump, an ancient iron range; and, more
promisingly, on a wooden table, a primus stove and a can of paraffin.
Outside, a small square yard held a woodshed, coal bin and tidy rustic privy.

The second door opened on to a steep stairway leading up into
another long room overhead, unfurnished except for a pile of mattresses
beside the fireplace.   Like the attic in "La Bohème"; but empty and silent.

Eager to be outside, she sluiced the
tea-things sketchily under the pump, took a pocketful of biscuits and set off
down the riverside path, picking her way over twisted tree-roots and slippery
rocks, past dripping thickets of spindle and hazel, and a spinney of little
Christmas trees.   A holly tree, thick with berries, shone through the mist,
and she thought childishly-a pity I shan't be here for Christmas.

She had come a long way when the river dwindled to hide itself in a
deep gully.   Dwarf oaks clung to the banks, their roots arching and
spreading to form mossy caverns where water voles or otters might find
shelter.   The path turned away to run uphill along the edge of the wood.

Ahead, as she climbed, the mist shone with a red-gold glow from
the east, like firelight seen through flimsy curtains; then dissolved and rolled
away.   At the top she looked down through clear bright air over fields
sloping seaward.   The sun's upper rim, breaking through low dark cloud,
made a dazzling crescent reflected in the ocean.

I with the morning's love have oft made sport;
And, like a forester, the groves may tread
Even till the eastern gate, all fiery-red,
Opening on Neptune with fair blessed beams,
Turns into yellow gold his salt-green streams...

She remembered hearing that Great-grandfather Dane, a forester, had loved
those lines; though he lived far from the sea, in the beechwoods of
Oxfordshire.   Now, turning downhill, she wondered where Shakespeare
might have come to the edge of a wood and seen that ocean sunrise.   But in
his day perhaps - when a squirrel could cross England in the treetops - there
would have been many such places, with forests stretching down to the sea.

The path ran through a pasture where sheep were huddled together - the first she had seen since that long-ago evening at Hendon. They lifted their heads to stare as she passed, shuffling back a pace, as though their fleeces were too heavy with dew for more than token retreat. She saw that the fields below were planted with rows of sprouting bulbs or dim low-growing crops of some sort. Further off lay a wide expanse of leafy green, and the breeze brought a thrilling scent of violets.

But the shore was still some way off: and she was due in the coroner's court at Farmouth. She made her way back, and followed the path upstream from the orchard, out to a twisting lane, and on to find St. Max station. This time she was in luck; a train was due, and she reached Farmouth town hall, a grey stone house by the quay, in good time for the inquest.

A women visitor, crossing a street, had been struck by a car and killed instantly, with such injuries that Rowan felt she could never again step lightly off a pavement into traffic. But how quickly one forgot: she found herself doing so, without a thought, as soon as she left the hall.

The victim was a teacher at a well-known girls' school; so there would be a few lines in some London papers. Back in Jamie's hut by Faro station, she found a list of addresses left ready, put through the Fleet Street calls, then banged out copies for various weeklies, local and scholastic.

Coming back from the post office, she bought a sandwich and sat on the doorstep in calm sunlight; listening to one or two trains, to the peal of a thrush, chirping of sparrows, the rustle of brown leaves drifting from a horse-chestnut tree overhead, and the rap of chestnut husks on the roof. The hut stood beside a grassy bank where spikes of scarlet berries grew. Jamie, she thought, must be the only journalist in England with conkers and cuckoo-pints at his office door.

He didn't appear, and soon her thoughts turned to the cottage, not yet seen properly by daylight. She was setting out in search of a bus to St. Max when a long black car drew up and a man in a dark suit leaned out to say politely:

"Jamie thought you'd like a lift down there?"

An undertaker; bound for the village inn at St. Max to take the late landlord on his last journey. Driving fast, they soon reached the scene of yesterday's baby drama, spun past the gates of Sheepskin House and turned into a lane that wound uphill through the woods. She was set down by a stone stile where, the man told her, a path led down to the orchard house.

She watched the hearse glide on at more decorous speed. A bell began to toll from the distant church tower. A shop across the road had its shutters up. Beside it stood a telephone box, and on impulse she went in and dialled the press room numbers in London, one after another, hoping to hear a familiar voice. But, at this busy hour, they were all engaged. And Caro wouldn't be home for hours ... still, she tried the Highgate number, and let it ring for a bit, then hung up and went slowly back to the stile.

The funeral bell had stopped. The mild bright afternoon was still, except for the chekkering of a jackdaw on a chimney, and the far-off wail of a seagull. Away to the south a calm sea gleamed like dull silver or mother-of-pearl. Framed in treetops, the grey harbour town seemed to float like a mirage on the horizon. The steep woods below were filled with misty gold light from spreading boughs: sycamore, oak, ash, beech; butter-yellow, buff-coloured, lemon, russet. But the river valley must already be in shadow. Soon it would be nightfall again.

She shivered, feeling a pang of homesickness - not for London now, but, quite unexpectedly, for Nine Wells and her family; for the familiar paddocks and horses, the front drive where she knew every beech and sycamore trunk by touch, the house with its sunny glass porch scented by Grandmother's verbenas and freesia; the old welcoming smells inside, peat fires, lamp oil, dog; the big kitchen at breakfast time, with cats purring, bacon frizzling, pots simmering on the range - hens' potatoes, mash for horses, new greengage jam in summer, marmalade in winter; the pleasure of pouring thick chill cream from an old yellow jug on to smoking hot porridge. *So what am I doing here?* she wondered. It's my holiday, I can go where I like. I can be at Euston tonight, in Ireland tomorrow. No need to stay on in that queer dark little house.

But no, she realised: I really don't want to see *them* again. Not yet. I was right about that before.

Besides ... this place was in a way her own, a new venture; a step away from her new friends as well as family, childhood and the outgrown past.

And, yes, someone had clearly taken quite a lot of trouble to get it ready for her. So - one more night here, at least?

25

Plunging downhill through the woods, she stopped short when a glossy cock pheasant sauntered out of cover on to the path below, scrabbling among the leaves until it found a sweet-chestnut husk to peck at, spilling out three nuts - a fat red one in the middle, a skimpy white runt on either side - and devouring them at leisure.

From here she could see the tops of the orchard trees, with one or two apple rinds and dull green leaves; and the end wall of the house, like a small stone barn tucked into the hillside.

Coming down to the house, she found a chip basket on the door latch, secured by a loop of string; holding a bottle of milk, a loaf wrapped in a napkin, a packet of bacon rashers. The unseen helper had been here again.

She glanced quickly round, looking for some retreating figure. No one was there; but what she saw made her gasp in amazement and stand there gazing, exclaiming aloud,

"No! It can't be -"

And then -

"But it *is*. It must be .. the very same place ... "

She was looking down at a picture she had known all her life; a green clearing, a little orchard, enclosed by autumn woods; the river beyond, the bridge with its curving parapet, the white feather of a waterfall below; and, on the far bank, the stone folly, the rowan tree, the high dark trees and tawny beeches of the wild garden. A real picture, a painting of Lizzie's that had hung in her Chelsea studio as long as Rowan could remember; with another, of a mysterious lion, pale greenish-gold, heraldic-looking, couchant in a rocky cave. Both pictures belonged to Ralph. She'd given them to him when he was a child, and now they must be in New Zealand ... but the first was here in front of her eyes, complete in every detail but one, and that one she'd met just now on the path above: a cock pheasant, a dab of russet paint with specks of scarlet, blue and white.

So Lizzie had been here at some time! An odd coincidence. Odder still because, so far as Rowan knew, she'd never set foot in Cornwall. On their journeys together they'd come no further west than Exmoor. It must have happened long ago - perhaps before she herself was born; yet now the place looked just the same. I'll write to her at once, she thought, and tell her I'm here, and ask when she came.

The sun had dipped behind the furthest trees, the picture was fading with the daylight; but she could hardly bear to leave it yet, her discovery seemed so odd and unexpected. She wandered down to the water. On a low twisted thorn tree near the bridge her eye caught a flutter of scarlet. A robin? No: a loop of ribbon tied to a twig. Looking closer, she saw that another twig held a circlet of blue beads, a child's bracelet; and she remembered the small face she'd seen last night at the window.

Dry reeds and hemlocks swayed and rustled on the far bank. One could almost fancy someone hiding, whispering and watching; and the gurgle of water over rocks seemed to echo a childish giggle. She called tentatively, "Hullo!" and again, "Hullo?" Silence. A robin ticked at her, then whistled softly; an owl called from the woods. She turned away to take refuge indoors, relighting the fire, filling the kettle, finding a toasting-fork by the hearth and toasting a rasher over the flames, then folding it into a slice of bread and butter. The taste was smoky but appetising. She pronged another rasher and propped it over the fire.

The light was gone from the windows, and again the fireside became a cave of flickering gleams and shadows; again, in the spreading warmth, the cricket set up its companionable chirping. Outside, the owls were crying up and down the valley.

She had left the door ajar; and suddenly a new sound made her turn and listen intently. Light sharp footfalls, tapping and clicking on the steps outside the door. Like a child in nailed boots, walking on tiptoe?

The steps reached the door, and paused; and there was another unnerving silence. She called, "Who's there?" and heard her voice falter.

The door was slowly pushed wider. There was a low snuffling like the sound she'd heard last night, and something showed itself for a moment, then retreated. A hairy muzzle; the tips of two large ears. She sprang up, thinking insanely, Not a *wolf*! - grabbed at the poker, and waited, poised between attack and flight.

Then a little grey donkey stepped delicately over the threshold, came up to the table and stood eying her and the dish of apples with engaging confidence.

As she fed him and stroked him, more steps approached outside. She looked round, expecting another donkey - and heard a cough, then a gentle knock, and found her second visitor waiting on the threshold. An elderly man, dark-suited and spruce, like the undertaker - no doubt he'd been to the funeral. He ducked his head in greeting, removing an ancient bowler hat; at the same time, she noticed, slipping her a very shrewd and inquisitive look. Then he caught sight of the donkey.

"Ah, the greedy good-for-nothing! Get him out of there, miss!"

But the sharp words were spoken in mild accents, and the donkey strolled out as calmly as he had come in, evading a token clout.

"Dick Monk, miss. From the lodge. If there's anything I can do for you -?" His shy manner failed to hide another gleam of curiosity.

"Oh! The house - someone got it ready - can you tell me who?"

He said evasively, "They told me you'd be coming."

"Well, look, I must pay you - for the food and everything."

He brushed this aside, murmuring, "No, no, that's all seen to. Yes, yes. All paid for."

"But -"

Again he muttered something. She caught the words 'agent' and 'Farmouth', but spoken so dismissively that she couldn't go on. Obviously, Arran Green wanted to keep his arrangements to himself? - no doubt to avoid being thanked. That was something she'd have to deal with when she was back in London. (Yes, and she'd have to explain, as tactfully as possible, why she hadn't stayed longer.)

"So - you're all alone, miss? And - how long will you be staying?"

"Well ... tonight anyway." Something made her add quickly, "But I love it here."

His face changed. He almost smiled, his blue eyes lighting up. His gaze travelled round the room, then back to her. He said slowly,

"I was born in this house."

"Were you!"

"Lived here as a boy. The old pheasantry, it was then. My father was head keeper, more than forty years. Spring time, we'd raise the birds out there on the grass ... "

"Pheasants? ... yes, I saw one up in the woods ... "

"Still a few left. Not many. Foxes clearing them out, with the rabbits gone." Dropping his air of reserve, he talked fluently for some minutes about the rabbit plague, myxomatosis, that had emptied the warrens and left the predators hungry. Now he seemed so approachable that she said impulsively -

"I wonder ... did you ever meet an artist here? Letty Izard?"

He blinked and looked away, shaking his head; put out, she could see, by the interruption. But, having begun, she persisted,

"She's my aunt. And she must have painted a picture here - the river, and the bridge, and the orchard - " (How amazing if Lizzie had actually stayed in this house, with this old fellow's parents!)

But now he was stiff and shy again, as though offended; backing away, not meeting her eye. A moment later he was gone. And she'd learned nothing.

Yet she had a clear impression of his look when she'd said 'Letty Izard'; a flash of awareness, before his face went blank.

26

She woke next morning still thinking of Lizzie, still meaning to write to her at once; but early sunlight, and the thought of the sea, drew her away again to the riverside path.

The morning was clear and fresh, as mild as September. A few late flowers bloomed on here and there - forget-me-nots, water mint, pink and silver mallows - and the cries of great-tits and thrushes rang through the woods. Walking quickly, she soon passed yesterday's landmarks, the Christmas trees, the holly, the sheep-fold; made her way through the fields, and came out on to a wide breezy grassland that gave way to a tangle of gorse and blackthorn at the cliff edge, where a track led to a steep sandy slide above the beach. A van was parked in the distance, and she saw someone approaching, and looked to see if it might be Peter Thoransen; but this was a stranger, a loiterer, prowling along by the bushes, then vanishing into cover when he looked back and saw her. A rabbit-catcher perhaps? But the rabbits were gone. She turned to the slide, sat down and took off, landing on a pile of dry black seaweed at the foot of the cliff.

She was in a little cove, horseshoe shaped, shut in at either point by high rocks. The tide was out; salt-white sands stretched away to glittering green water topped with foam. Under the cliff, a line of sea wrack showed that the cove must be filled at high tide. The seaweed held a jumble of oddments, shells, crab claws, feathers, bits of driftwood, sanded, bleached and twisted into curious shapes: antlers, antennae, branching corals, a wishbone, a pregnant nymph, a stringless lute ... she seemed to have been there only a few minutes, roving up and down; but suddenly the sea was much nearer, and running in fast. The slide she'd come down was too steep and slippery to scramble up, the cliffs too sheer for climbing. She would have to make her way over the rocks to the open beach and sandhills on the other side.

Passing a gash in the cliff, the entrance to a cave, she saw lines of animal footprints leading in and out; paw marks with broad pads and the dint of sharp claws, outlined on firm sand. Badger prints. The beach around was criss-crossed with more prints, and littered with pink and white shellfish fragments. One low flat rock was ringed with paw marks, as though the badgers had played games there by moonlight.

Long ago, on a country expedition, she and Ralph had spent a night out of doors in the New Forest, and awakened to find a badger watching them. Would *he* remember that? She could dash back to the house, fetch her camera, take pictures of these beautiful paw-prints, and send him one.

But she realised - there wouldn't be time. Long before she could return, the cove would be under water. Still, she could stay another night and come back tomorrow; the badgers would be out again tonight. Where were they now, she wondered. There might be a sett at the back of this cave, above the high water mark: those inward footprints might be made by homing badgers, not roving crab-hunters. She would have liked to take a look inside; but already the quiet treacherous current was swirling along the nearest rocks. Soon there would be deep water everywhere, she would have to swim ... She retreated hastily, splashing through the shallows and scrambling over the reef, cutting her hands on razor-edged shells, to reach the wide bay where the tide seemed to advance at a gentle pace, with no threat of danger. Seagulls stood along the beach, waiting like children for the foam to wash over their feet.

Back on the riverside path, she recalled seeing a tide-table yesterday in the window of the village shop, and made her way there to study it.

The shop was open today, and inside she found Peter Thoransen being served with loaves and fishes and other provisions by a brisk little woman who appeared to be sympathising with him over some looming crisis. Waiting her turn, Rowan gathered that most of his workers would be away tomorrow on some jaunt: and so how would be manage for pickers, she cried, wrapping up a pair of kippers and fixing him with a needling look that betrayed more relish than concern. He remained calm, hardly exerting himself to answer. Then, turning to leave, he saw Rowan and stopped short, staring at her in obvious surprise.

Because I'm still here, she guessed; he never thought I'd last two nights, down there by myself.

Recovering, he gave her a brief nod and escaped with his armful of rations. As the door was shutting, she remembered their eventful drive and ran out to ask,

"That mother! - did you ever hear what happened?"

He looked puzzled for a moment, then remembered too:

"Oh ... yes ... she was all right. Just in time. The father rang to thank me. Decent of him."

When he smiled, she thought, he was really rather striking. She hesitated, watching as he stowed his things in the van, and suddenly heard herself asking -

"Those pickers ... that you won't have tomorrow ... what were they supposed to pick? I mean - " she added recklessly - "I just wondered - could I help?"

"You!" He looked astounded. "Aren't you working for Jamie Cameron?"

It was her turn to show surprise. His faint grin suggested *Things get about*, and she brought him up to date:

"Not now. I'm on holiday. I just thought - it would be a change ... " A change from hearing how people came to their death.

"H'm." He seemed sceptical. "It's flower-picking. Field work. You've never done any?"

"Not that sort," she admitted.

84

"So? Then what sort?"

"Oh ... harvesting, a bit. And picking strawberries - "

That seemed to go down a little better. He nodded and became business-like.

"Very well. Come if you like. Hard work, you know. Back-aching. Cold out there. Start at first light."

She waited to hear what and where.

"Anemones. You know what they are?"

"I think so."

"All right. You go along by the river - through the water woods - and it's the top field, the first you come to." He eyed her thoughtfully.

"I won't put you on piece-work, you wouldn't make your money. I'll give you - what are you, sixteen?"

"Eighteen!"

"Sorry. Two bob an hour? Picking and bunching. That's over the rate." He added carefully, "A bit over."

"Yes. Right."

"Here you are." He reached into the van, scooped out two flat baskets and handed them over. "Start up at the top, work down to the shed, bunch in there. Eight to a bunch. OK?"

As he started up the van she called - "Won't *anyone* else be there?" and he called back, "Only a couple of - " *monks*, it sounded like. Lay brothers from some settlement? Brown robes and sandals?

No doubt she'd find out tomorrow.

She wondered ruefully what had possessed her, decided to back out, then compromised: *if* I wake up late, I'll just forget it.

27

She was awake before sunrise, lighting the primus, gulping coffee, wrapping up bread and cheese bought in readiness. She found an old pair of leaky gumboots in the kitchen, and clumped along by the river and up the woodside track, then down past the sheep to the top field; and , yes, these must be the anemones - row after row of low fronded foliage and flower buds, drab grey, faint pink or navy, as dingy and dusty-looking as she remembered. Would anyone buy such stuff? But that was the farmer's affair. She set out to pick the buds, stripping the first two rows beside the path and piling them into both baskets.

Feet and fingers were quickly soaked with dew, then frozen, then numb. She longed for the sun to appear and bring daylight, if not warmth. Today there was no fiery sunrise, only low cloud and mist, and the boom of a fog-horn out at sea. When she had worked for an hour or so the air was dank and chill as ever, the landscape shrouded in vapour that sometimes dissolved for a moment, showing the sun as a disc of cold silver just above the horizon. Sometimes, too, the ground-mist would drift and part, giving her a glimpse of two dark shapes away to her left, bent over distant rows; whether men or women, pickers or stray sheep, she could hardly tell.

The anemone buds had no scent, but again she smelt violets from the field below. Presently, as the mist thinned a little, she caught sight of two dimly lighted squares like cottage windows, and came to the door of a wooden shack, furnished inside with trestle tables and buckets of water, and lit by two hanging lanterns.

A women wearing mud-coloured dungarees over many wraps stood at one of the tables, tying up bunches with green twine and trimming the stalks with scissors, while an elderly man packed the flowers into boxes. As Rowan came in he gave her a brief stare, but the woman made no sign.

She tipped her load out on to a table, collected scissors and twine from a shelf and set to work; but her fingers were too numb for speed. When a boy sidled in, also laden, the woman greeted him with a loud sniff and a derisive - "Oh, dodging school now, is it?" He thumbed his nose, retorting, "Sucks, ma - half term," and the man rebuked him sourly - "That isn't how to speak to your mother, Chad Monk." Silence fell once more, but the atmosphere now seemed charged with hidden discord. The boy took the table next to hers and watched her efforts with a sidelong grin while deftly clearing his own pile. She got on better when the Monks were gone, and began to feel almost expert until the old packer came over to scoop up her bucketful with a grunt - "This *all*?"

The woman hadn't seemed to notice Rowan; but late in the day they had an odd encounter.Alone in the shed again, she found her scissors too damp to cut the twine, and borrowed a pair from Mrs. Monk's table, so new and sharp that she could cut a handful of strings in a moment. Returning the scissors, she looked up to see their owner coming in, and began to explain - but the words died before a scowl so malevolent that she could only back away. It was a relief when Peter Thoransen drove up to collect the boxes, and the day was over.

Stumbling back through the woods, weary and chilled, she thought of last summer's heat wave, and how they had all complained about it. In town, one expected to be sheltered from the weather; people working all the year round in the fields no doubt expected as a matter of course to be too hot or cold, soaked by rain or pinched by frost. Next week, back in the courts, this day of rustic toil would seem remote from normal life.

Eager to be indoors out of the mist and gloom, she quickened her pace, and her gumboot suddenly slithered and trapped itself between two stones. She fell headlong, giving her foot a sharp wrench, and almost crushing the pocketful of anemone buds she had rescued from a rubbish-bin. The homeward plod became a painful limp. But soon she was home, warm and dry again; drinking hot soup, toasting kippers, describing her day in flippant letters to Lizzie and Sarah. Her ankle still hurt when she tried to walk, but she told herself it was nothing - by morning she would be all right.

28

But she was far from all right. The ankle had swollen alarmingly, and any movement brought crippling stabs of pain. She had a moment of fright - no telephone, no likely caller: how was she to escape? - then made up her mind not to flap. She could rest today and bathe her foot, and tomorrow it *must* be better.

This was not in any case a day for her sea walk, or for taking photographs. The wind had risen, sweeping away the mist and driving dark rain-clouds from the sea. Shut in with her thoughts, indolent after yesterday's labours and a restless night, she lay on the couch in a kind of waking trance, watching the river and the shifting firelight. Sudden rainstorms lashed the windows, blotting out the view that Lizzie had painted in calm autumnal sunshine. When Liz answered her letter, she would know *which* autumn.

And, after all, she was glad there was no telephone. The ringing would have been an intrusion into peaceful musing. 'Deep meditation' must begin like this - for hermits in grottos, St. Kevin in his cell at Glendalough, St. Jerome in the wilderness with that guardian lion, copied by Lizzie from some Durer work - the other picture she'd given Ralph. One day, 'down under', she would see both paintings again.

Outside, trees tossed and roared, and sometimes a whirling twig rapped sharply on the glass. In this warm firelit cavern the only sounds were the whisper of flames, an occasional chirp from the cricket, the soft purr and fizzle of logs sinking down on to ashes, the rasp of a mouse sharpening its teeth somewhere. It struck her that this solitude and silence, so rare in her own life, must have been commonplace to her country forebears: to the forester's wife, and Scots women like Grandfather Izard's mother, in lonely Border farmhouses, with the men away looking after their flocks on the hills, or at sheep fairs, or perhaps - in remoter times - on more dubious excursions; those Border raids and feuds and forays that Scott had heard about as a youth in shepherds' kitchens. Great-grandmother Izard had her own link with that romantic past. She could claim descent from a namesake, another Katherine Douglas: brave 'Kate Barlass', who had tried to hold a door fast, thrusting her frail arm through the bolt sockets, while the king fled from his enemies.

Grandfather's first wife Minnie, from another Border home, seemed to have grown up in a less rugged ambience. Her father had enjoyed collecting and studying moths; and she, a gifted self-taught artist, had left a sketch-book recording some of his favourites in pastels or water-colours, passing on her talent to her youngest daughter Letty: later known as Lizard from her signature, L. Izard. Still, there was nothing of the frail or whimsical female artist about either of them. Minnie was a keen horsewoman, strong and dashing enough to drive four-in-hand; and Lizzie had been an air raid warden in the London blitz.

Rowan knew a good deal about these Scottish relations from Aunt Lizard; and about her English forebears from Father, on long country walks when she was a child. At fifteen, she had actually planned to 'break away' and live in some woodland retreat: taking after her other great-grandfather, the poetry-reading forester. He had had brains and might have used his expert knowledge to make money in the timber trade, but heart and mind were set in another direction: he wanted simply to spend his life in the woods. Ralph, with the same ambition, had found his own way to do that. But she herself had changed; now she was glad this was only an interlude, that she would be back in London on Sunday and in the press room at Westminster on Monday. No doubt the same urge to escape to different scenes had drawn her mother and Lizzie away from County Kildare to London, and Aunt Rose to China with Ralph's father.

Nor were they the first of her elders to go East. Years before, the forester's eldest son had been a missionary in China; where, according to family legend, he founded a school for orphans and was honoured by the old Empress with the Order of the Green Dragon. A younger brother, Grandfather Dane, leaving home in turn, had travelled no further than Kent, crossing the Thames to become manager of a country estate. Here the legend involved a frequent visitor, a relation of Madame Tussaud, who would enthuse over camellias and orchids in the glasshouses - "So exquisite. *Just like wax.*" At the end of the century, however, that part of rural Kent had been swallowed up by London, vanishing as completely as the ancient oak wood from which the estate took its name. In the new suburbs, not even a street name kept its memory alive. Late in life, Grandfather had seen the old camellia trees flaunting their waxen rose and white through the roof of a derelict glasshouse, before the levellers moved in.

At that time, wealthy company directors would recruit young clerks from their country estates. So some of the forester's descendants found themselves in City offices, *the green thumb to the ledger knuckled down.* Others, except for one dedicated gardener, took up teaching or journalism, or became draughtsmen in a leading firm that made war weapons. One of these later joined the team behind the grim 'dam-busting' bombs of the second world war. A far cry from the forest: but his rare wartime leaves were spent in the country, hay-making or splitting logs. At heart perhaps they were all exiles rather than escapers.

Perhaps I am too, she thought. It's true what I told Dick Monk - I love it here. In a way, I'll be quite sorry to leave.

29.

By morning the storm had passed. Saturday brought fine weather; and an early visitor, the foraging donkey. Giving him her last apple, she realised with dismay that the ankle was still swollen and painful. She couldn't attempt to stand on it, let alone put on a shoe; walking was out of the question. It was all she could do to struggle as far as the kitchen, then the yard, using a broom for a crutch. But somehow she must get up the hill to post her letters, buy food for today and book a taxi for tomorrow.

The donkey nuzzled her empty hands in reproach. She put an arm round his warm shaggy neck, and it dawned on her that he might make himself useful. Slipping her scarf round his neck, she hopped beside him to the door, coaxed him down the steps, mounted and nudged him towards the path. He made no objection: ambled quietly uphill, brushed through a gap beside the stile and delivered her at the shop just as it was being unlocked.

A beach donkey in summer, the shopkeeper told her: astray from Sheepskin Farm, where a troop of them passed the winter.

"Can't keep old Peregrine in. They never know where he's to. Always out and about, rummaging and cadging."

Then she exclaimed over Rowan's sprain, handing out advice and embrocation, eggs and mushrooms, with apples and other bribes for Peregrine. The donkey waited on the door sill, tapping one hoof impatiently, until he was shoved aside by a boy who bounded in, slammed down a tray of anemone bunches on the counter, scattering everything else, sang out - "Watch it, Ma Lilypot," and escaped before she could retort, "I'll tell your dad of you, Chad Monk!"

Everyone, it seemed, had it in for this uncouth boy. But the shopkeeper hinted, "Oh well ... can you wonder? Bert Monk got out before he was born, and poor Dotty Monk ... not that I'd say a word against her," she amended hastily; adding with a half-laugh, "Safer not, I believe. Supposed to be a witch of some kind - "

"No?"

"So they say. Get across her and you're in trouble. Oh, nothing deadly - toothache, it might be, or falling off a bike - "

Or twisting your ankle? Rowan thought, recalling that queer look.

At noon gnats were dancing over the river, and a flock of martins appeared, dashing up and down the banks, feeding and piping; late travellers, temple-haunting martlets perhaps from the far north. Sunlight slanted across the windows, rousing the mouse, the cricket and other lodgers. A bluebottle lurched about the room, an earwig climbed out of a filbert husk, a great spider crept from shadow to shadow on the floor, a ragged tortoiseshell butterfly drifted and fluttered; a queen wasp came out of

91

hiding to beat on the window, avid to escape into the sunshine, with no sense of the murderous cold night ahead. Woodwork creaked in the faint warmth, and once, half dreaming, she fancied that ghostly footfalls stole to and fro in the room overhead. Like Mariana, like the moated grange:

All day within the dreaming house
The doors upon their hinges creaked.
The blue fly sung in the pane, the mouse
Behind the something wainscot squeaked
Or from the crevice peered about.
Old footsteps trod the upper floors,
Old voices called her from without ...

Aunt Lizard's voice especially. Lizzie, in fact, had been in her thoughts ever since she saw the orchard house - even before she recognised the setting for that picture: no doubt because they had been together so often in other country places.

In the kitchen, when she got herself out there to the primus, a centipede rippled like a sandy cat in a shaft of light from the doorway, and scurrying woodlice curled at a touch into silver-grey berries. A beetle had hung itself up on the wall by the sink; its wing case, elegantly scalloped, had a greenish-golden sheen like ash buds in April. Back on her couch, forking up a plateful of fried eggs and baked beans, rough-and-ready but hot and filling, she thought idly - how beautiful things are, when you've time to look at them: the filbert in its husk, pine and cedar cones in the log-box, a dark pink mushroom ringed with ivory, her saucerful of anemones, so drab looking yesterday, now a flourish of brilliant blue and vermilion ... an apple leaf, lime-green, heart -shaped - a snowy feather out on the grass - a thistle flower under the window, visited by darting glittering insects ... no wonder architects and decorators so often copied nature. That little folly, for instance, across the river: the dome shaped like a button mushroom, the high window alcoves pointed like willow leaves.

Then something else caught her eye. Someone was coming down the slope from the trees, past the folly, over the bridge; a nurse in uniform cloak, on her way to the shop perhaps, or to catch a bus in the village. She passed out of sight among the orchard trees. But then there were footsteps outside, a tap on the door, a voice calling, "Hallo there!"

The latch was lifted and a face appeared: pert and freckled, framed in pale red hair. Rowan started up, crying: "Bridie!"

She was Bridie Hanlon. Lily Hanlon's sister.

Lily had been Rowan's childhood companion at Nine Wells during the war, and afterwards in London, until she married. Bridie, training to be a nurse, had come over two years ago to a London hospital, and sometimes stayed with Rowan when her parents were away.

"Bridie, how *weird* - what *are* you doing here?"

"Midwifery, what else? And you?"

Rowan sank back, wincing. "Spraining my ankle, for one thing."

"Yes, so we heard."

"You heard! Whoever from?"

Bridie shrugged. "We'd word from the lodge, I think it was - would someone take a look at you."

"Oh, the lodge ... "Dick Monk, then. And the shopkeeper must have told him. (Or someone else - one of those unseen watchers she'd imagined by the river?)

"Well now, let's see." Bridie threw off her cloak, sat down by Rowan and fingered the swelling. "Not much wrong with that." She fetched water, produced a bandage, did a little brisk mopping and binding, chatting away meanwhile.

"So Miss Lizzie - Mrs. Oliver - so they married out there? And a little boy, and at her age, mind you - isn't that grand?"

"Yes, grand ... Bridie, what on earth brings you down *here*? Miles from London?"

Another shrug. "Well, I'd always a fancy to see this place, you know - "

Rowan interrupted -

"Oh, but listen, I'll tell you something queer. Lizzie must have been here once! She painted the view from this house - look, look out there! Do you see? I wonder when she came?"

Bridie's hands were still for a moment. She raised her head and gave Rowan a long stare. For once, she seemed at a loss for any reply. Her cheeks grew bright, her sharp grey-green eyes widened; her lips parted, but no words came. After a pause she shook her head, dropped her eyes and went on with her ministrations. Of course - Rowan thought - paintings had meant nothing to her sister either. Lily had always spoken of Lizzie's 'copying'.

She persisted - "I didn't know she'd ever been in Cornwall ... oh *thanks*, that's much better - "

"There now. You can try walking a bit tomorrow, no harm."

"I'll have to anyway. I'm going home."

Again Bridie looked at her closely. "But - you might be back? Or will they be letting the house again?"

"This house? Has it been let, then?"

"They say so. Some of the nurses stayed here once. Great parties they'd have ... " Bridie spoke absently, still watching Rowan, who became aware of busy curious thoughts buzzing somewhere behind that bland gaze, and launched resignedly into explanations: the lawyer's letter, the barrister friend who must have arranged her visit. Bridie made no comment, but her face changed. She had seemed guarded, puzzled, preoccupied in some way;

now she wore a faint knowing smirk. No doubt, like Sarah, she had views about kindly old benefactors. Refusing to be drawn in that direction, Rowan began to tell her about Far News and the second inquest. A good move: Bridie stopped smirking and seized on the medical evidence, picking over Rowan's sketchy recollection and adding details from her own experience. Presently she got up and began to prowl about, scanning the place with keen interest, taking a look upstairs, dating the mattresses up there from the nurses' time, when half a dozen might camp here together; fetching more wood from the shed, then strolling back to the kitchen - "I'll make us some tea, shall I?" Too impatient to wait for the water to boil, she was soon back with brimming cups afloat with tea-leaves.

"See? That means strangers coming. They'll keep you amused, so."

Looking out of the window, she added,

"Didn't I tell you? One of them here already." She wandered to the door, opened it, eyed the new arrival and shot Rowan a look that said as blithely as Juliet's Nurse - *A man, young lady! And such a man!*

As well she might. He was Peter Thoransen.

He strode in, gave them both a curt nod, told Rowan, "I brought your money," tossed a buff envelope on to the table, glanced at the bandaged ankle, muttered something - sympathetic, perhaps? - and departed, shutting the door with a snap.

Bridie mocked, "Sorry. I scared him off. Wait now, he'll be back." She stood by the window, watching him march away down the river path.

"Smashing, isn't he? I've seen him in the gardens up above." She yawned and looked at her watch. "Must be off, I'll be missing breakfast."

"Night duty?"

"Yes, and that's when the little beggars start arriving. And no staff hardly."

"But I saw a lot of nurses, a whole coach-load - "

"Day shift, yes. They decamp and leave us to it - one staff nurse and yours truly."

"Suppose a lot of infants come at once - how do you cope?"

"Well may you ask. One of these nights there'll be a disaster." But Rowan didn't believe her. Bridie was a great one for drama.

Still, she'd been right about the visitors. She was hardly out of sight when there came more footsteps, another knock, a loud halloo -

"Anyone home? Of course you are," said Jamie, walking in. "Well, well. Met with a mishap, haven't we?"

"Goodness, how did *you* hear?"

"My spies," he said vaguely; and then, with a rush -

"Look. I've been having a word with my pa. Do you think you could stay on - just for a week or two, till I find myself a partner?"

94

30

On Tuesday morning the coroner's court at Farmouth was packed for an inquest that, as it opened, seemed to be a straightforward road accident inquiry. 'Nothing special,' as Jamie had put it: if sudden violent death could ever be so described. But, fetching her early, helping her limp up the hill to his car, he explained -

"The thing is - there's a rumour going round. Worth taking a look, I thought."

They had both been busy yesterday at a public inquiry in Faro about a cliff top pathway; today, instead, she was sharing a seat with Pip Saunders, the amiable gray-haired editor of the Farmouth News.

A youth from St. Max, cycling fast down a steep winding road at night, had crashed into an approaching car and broken his neck. The car had been driven by a stranger from another county. Looking white and wretched, he told the court that, as he drove round a bend, the bicycle "seemed to come from nowhere" and struck the car head on, throwing the rider into the air. They had got him to hospital, but were told that he was dead. Questioned, he said he'd seen no light on the bicycle. The cyclist had "taken the corner wide" and slewed across the road into the car. "He just came straight at me. There was nothing I could do. It all happened in a flash."

From somewhere in the crowd a voice called out "No!" and was hushed.

The driver's wife, speaking almost inaudibly, said she had seen the bicycle for one second only in the car headlights, before the crash. Shuddering at the memory, she looked down to hide her face.

"Which side of the road was your car when this happened?"

She murmured something, looking ready to faint.

The coroner admonished her, "Please speak up, madam. I know this is very distressing, but we must hear your evidence."

He repeated his question: "Which side-?"

The clock ticked loudly through eight seconds before she whispered, "I can't - I don't - he *must* have been on his wrong side, mustn't he?"

Again the voice shouted "No!" Then a youth was standing up, shoving his way forward, jerking out angry sentences. The coroner's officer went to meet him; but before he could be calmed and put in the witness box he yelled at the top of his voice,

"That's all lies. All lies! We were right there in the wood, me and Linda - we saw it happen, the whole thing. It was *him*" - shaking his raised fist at the driver - "he came round that corner, top speed, on his wrong side. Fred never had a chance ..."

The coroner began to speak. Again he was interrupted, this time by the driver's wife; and this time the court heard every word. She cried out,

"Yes, that's true. *We* were on our wrong side. My husband- he took that corner blind, it's one of his tricks, *he does it to frighten me* ..." She burst into wild sobs and ran from the court.

Behind her, the shocked stillness was broken first by a long gasp from the crowd, then by a gabble of comment, and a few shouted threats. The driver sat open-mouthed, gazing about him with an air of total bewilderment. The coroner raised his voice to announce: "This inquest is adjourned."

" ... depart hence and take your ease," droned the usher. "God save the Queen."

"Depart hence and have a coffee,"Pip Saunders murmured. "Got your stick? Come along..."

In the coffee-shop Rowan exclaimed, "What will happen now!"

"Oh, he'll reopen with a jury, I suppose."

But she hadn't meant that. She was thinking of the husband and wife, and their fearful situation.

"Oh yes," Pip agreed. "Got a problem, haven't they?"

"But ... did you believe her?"

He said soberly, "The voice of truth? We hear it sometimes, don't we? Doesn't always cut much ice though."

"Especially," she wondered, "from a woman?"

"H'm, well ... we'll see next time. Unless," he added, "Jamie takes on that wag from Port Reith - then you'll be off, I expect?"

What wag?

It seemed that a journalist, a London man with an impressive record ("sort of unfrocked genius, we hear") had applied for a post as reporter on an evening paper further west, and arrived there for interview just as the editor received a last-minute warning from his London office - "Don't touch *him*, for God's sake. Never sober. Sacked from every paper in the Street." The applicant was met with embarrassed apologies, brushed them aside with an air - "Yes, yes, I quite understand, say no more sir, no hard feelings" - and proposed a friendly lunchtime drink before they parted. The editor accepted, and was seen no more that day. Rumour said he had been collected from some obscure pub late at night by the news editor.

The newcomer was next heard of on a small-town weekly paper, where he was offered a trial run in exchange for a solemn promise not to drink; but the venture failed for a different reason. His start in Fleet Street dated from a time when a bright copy-boy, given the chance of promotion, had plunged straight into national news. This late début as a parochial reporter brought surprises to him and his editor. He strolled back from petty sessions with a blank notebook: "No, old boy, nothing there. Not a line." And then, incredulously, "You can't mean you want drunks and bicycle lights!" On a routine call to the fire station he overlooked two items that duly appeared in the rival paper: "Blaze In Chip Shop" and "Hoax Call To

Old People's Home." A call at the hospital did produce three lines: a cyclist had been treated for bruises after a fall. He had collided with a badger in a dark lane. (No word, Rowan noticed, about the badger's injuries.) But, sent to visit a remote village where the site of a new street lamp was being debated, he again drew a blank; and later found himself gazing, bemused, at a lead story in the other paper: "Call for Light On Lovers' Lane. Den Of Vice, Says Councillor."

And then, in his second precarious week, he came to grief over an important event, the first night of "The Mikado" by the local operatic society. From this he turned in only a chatty interview with the producer ... "My dear chap, why didn't you tell me? Never dreamed you'd expect me to *sit through it*, Tit-bloody-Willow and all that, amateurs! ... a bit much damn it." The other paper had a double column giving every name in the programme, from Pooh Bah ("a brilliant performance") to scene-shifters, programme-sellers and providers of refreshments; and the defaulter sadly agreed to depart when his time was up.

"Amusing fellow, though," Pip said. "They all liked him. Monty would have kept him on, just for the laughs, but of course their directors wouldn't wear it."

"Sounds like a man I know in London. Derry Gillespie."

"But that's who he is!"

"He can't be! ... *Derry*? What's he doing in Cornwall!"

"Looking for a house, he says. If someone else takes a chance on him. Might suit Jamie ... so long as he keeps off the drink."

Rowan caught the next train to Faro: and found that Derry had got there first.

Jamie, whatever his misgivings, sympathised with him, laughed at the saga of his trials, and agreed rather warily that they might work together.

"But," he told Rowan in private, "I'd like you to stay another week, if you can bear it? Rest up next weekend, get your ankle right - then we'll see how the old boy makes out ... "

31

That evening Peter Thoransen put his head round the office door to offer her a lift home. After a silent drive, he remarked at the stile, "I'd better see you down?"

"Oh no, thanks. I'm all right now. Nearly."

"Still." He took her arm and marched down beside her to the door. She felt bound to offer tea; and was taken aback when he accepted, muttering "Well - perhaps," following her in, and lighting the fire for her while she was in the kitchen. He stood by the window as he drank, looking down at the river, and she found herself telling him about the decorated thorn tree by the bridge.

"Children playing about, I suppose - only I've never seen them. Just once, that is - "

Was he listening or not? She went on,

"Rather risky for them, isn't it? The river, I mean?"

"Not when it's as low as this. At flood times, yes. My mother tried to keep me away, when I was young."

"But - you weren't very near? Out at Woods Farm?"

He turned to look at her in surprise. "But we didn't live there then. We lived here."

"*Here*? You don't mean ... in this house?"

"Certainly. I was born here."

She stared at him. "I didn't know ... I thought ... Dick Monk said *they* used to?"

"Of course. But long before us."

"Then - why don't you now? Why did you leave?"

"We left when the war was coming. We went back."

"Back?"

"To Denmark."

She said again, "I didn't know ... You're Danish?"

"And English. I told you, I was born here. My father had Woods Farm for years."

Danish. That would account, she thought, for his blond looks, his unusual surname, his slight foreign accent, unlike the foreignness of Cornish speech.

"I came back after the war, as soon as I could."

"But ... not to this house?"

"I couldn't do that. It wasn't ours. It belongs to ... someone else."

"Someone named - Arran Green?"

That seemed to mystify him. He shook his head, looking at her intently, saying nothing.

"And your parents - they've stayed in Denmark?"

Still silence. At last he said,

"My father was killed. In the Resistance. Then my mother died."

He came over to put down his cup, adding quietly,

"I must go, I have to be at the church. St. Max Day today, did you know?"

"St. Max! You mean he's a proper saint? I'd never heard of him ... "

"He has other names, I think. A saint for fishermen. So we ring tonight."

She sat in the dark for a long time, listening to the distant bell music, the rustling trees, the waterfall, the call of owls up and down the river. When the bells stopped she lit a candle for company. Watching the flame, she was reminded of her first night here, and that strange dream, waiting for the cry of a newborn child. In this old house people must have waited for the birth of many infants: Peter himself, and Dick Monk and his brother, long ago, and how many more, back in the past? Beyond the glow of candlelight, the circle of familiar shadows, darkness seemed to press forward, crowded with other lives and memories.

32

Jamie's doubts about his new man were soon modified, if not laid to rest. On his first days with Far News, Derry tracked down and sold a couple of useful stories. With this fresh start he seemed to recover his old flair; and Jamie, reassured, was ready to condone his slapdash life-style, assuming that he would sort himself out before long.

He had turned up in an ancient car, loaded with carrier bags and battered suitcases which he dumped in a corner of the office. A local newsman, dropping in, eyed the sagging pile of baggage, the litter of old shoes and coats behind the door, the shaving things on the window-sill, and asked,

"Why doesn't the fellow take a room?"

"Oh well. Give him time. Hard up at the moment, he says."

"Can't see why. Only himself to keep?"

Jamie said drily, "I daresay there's a wife or two somewhere."

"Still - sleeping on the floor! Must be crazy."

"Only when he starts up that old banger. He drives like a drunk on the dodgems - beats me how he got down here at all."

Catching Rowan's eye, Jamie told her, "Don't you let him give you a lift anywhere!"

Forewarned, she did her best to take this advice; but that evening Derry saw her miss her bus, and would hear no refusal. As a non-driver, she rarely noticed other people's style; now she saw at once what Jamie meant. Talking nonstop, Derry swerved and skidded out of the town; once in the country he rattled into top speed, scraped past stone hedges, cut corners, overtook in the face of an oncoming lorry, narrowly missed collision with a tractor. Half-way to St. Max the headlamps failed, and he plunged on with flickering sidelights, never slackening speed until they drew up by the stile. She escaped, shaking. He called gaily,

"Pick you up in the morning. Eight-thirty, all right?" and roared away before she could answer. Grimly telling herself, *The pig got up at six o'clock*, she caught the first train to Faro. Derry, turning up later, greeted her with sunny reproach.

"Where did you get to, poppet?"

"Sorry, I - "

"Found my way down to your place. Couldn't make anyone hear. Thought you'd overslept!"

"Yes, well- "

"Nice little house. Just what I'm looking for myself. All on your own, are you?"

In the evening he knocked at the door. "Just thought I'd drop in. Come and have a drink somewhere? (Just tonic for me of course, on the wagon nowadays) ... "

She had started lighting a fire upstairs at night to dispel the damp and chill. Somehow she found herself showing him round the house. He glanced about appreciatively, accepted coffee and made himself agreeable, telling a string of new anecdotes. Preparing to leave, he repeated his offer to fetch her in the morning.

"No, Derry. Please don't trouble."

"No trouble. Not a bit. Pleasure."

When she shook her head he looked hurt and puzzled. "If you say so. All right if I drop by sometimes, though?"

He sounded so plaintive that she had to say, "Oh yes, of course."

A mistake. He was there again on Saturday. "Thought - just look you up, see you're all right."

The night was wet and stormy. He stood dripping by the hearth, looking rather flushed and shivery, like someone starting a cold. She said reluctantly,

"You do look wet. Better take off your coat?"

He did this very slowly, struggling with the buttons, and she saw that there was a bottle hidden under the coat. Also - she now realised - he smelled of whisky or brandy ... so he was drinking again. But only because of his cold?

She made tea and watched as he swallowed it at a gulp, setting the cup down on the table edge so that it fell on to the rug. He seemed not to notice this, but looked on as she picked it up and refilled it, murmuring vaguely,

"Kind girl. Never let a fellow down. Eh?"

He swayed, caught hold of her and wrapped her in a clumsy embrace. She hugged him briefly, not to seem unfriendly, and wondered how soon she might get rid of him. The rain had been beating on the windows; presently there was a lull.

"Derry, the rain's stopped. Hadn't you better get back?"

"Back," he repeated, as though in a daze. "Back where?"

"Well - wherever you're staying?"

"No room ... no room ... at inn. Stay here - all right, my darling? Doss down anywhere ... "

He slid to the hearth rug, shut his eyes and seemed to fall asleep on the instant. Or could he have *passed out*, she wondered? Then he began to snore thunderously ... so at least he was alive. She retreated upstairs with a rug and cushion, and lay awake by the fire for a long time, hearing the snores rise and fall, dreading the embarrassments of the morning - when they must both admit that he'd been helplessly drunk.

But Sunday morning revealed a transformation.

She woke to the smell of bacon frying, and found Derry in the kitchen, humming to himself, shaking the pan expertly over the primus. The bottle had disappeared. He must have been out to fetch a bag from his car -

103

so had he *planned* to stay here? Washed, brushed and shaved, in crisply laundered shirt-sleeves (another surprise) he greeted her kindly, spruce and genial as an elderly uncle. And that, it appeared, was the role he had in mind.

"Been thinking. Suppose I perch here for a night or two? Just till I find somewhere in town? Give you a hand - tough all by yourself, little thing like you. Lonely too I should think? Bit creepy after dark? What do you say?"

Not on your life. I like being on my own, thanks.

But this prompt answer found no voice. Trying to tone down the message, wondering too if he were really hard up, unable to afford a lodging - she hesitated, and was lost. Uncle Derry moved in, bag and baggage, and lasted for the rest of the week.

Once in, however, he gave very little trouble, as she admitted on the ' phone to Sarah. He allowed her to make her own way to and from work, and spent most of his evenings elsewhere. She hoped he was spending them in looking for a place of his own, so that she could finish her stay in happy solitude. It was true that she'd wished more than once for company - but for Ralph, for Sarah. And in one way his presence was awkward.

Dick Monk, coming in on Sunday afternoon with another tin of paraffin, was greeted by Derry in ebullient mood, and did not respond. His face took on a look of stony disapproval, and he left by the back way without a word. Next day, on her return, she made an odd discovery: a new bolt had been fitted inside the stairway door. Dick must have done this while the house was empty; but she had no chance to comment, as he didn't call again.

The shopkeeper, Mrs. Lilypot, had also changed, serving Rowan in absent-minded silence very unlike her former chatty curiosity. And Derry, strolling in with her for cigarettes, attempting another spot of camaraderie, made no headway at all. Clearly they were causing a mild scandal. Just as well they'd be gone so soon.

Jamie, preoccupied with work and a new girl friend, knew nothing of all this. Rowan's ankle was better, but she still walked cautiously, and when possible he left her to spend unexacting days with typewriter and telephone. Derry meanwhile kept down his powerful thirst with tea and coffee, and followed up various news items competently enough, though without the panache of his early successes. If Jamie suspected him of off-duty drinking, he said nothing yet; and Rowan, asleep upstairs by the time her lodger returned, was thankful to find him at breakfast-time as presentable and anxious to please as on his first morning.

She was to leave on the following Monday, and on Saturday night she waited up for Derry, to remind him that his stay must end next day. It occurred to her that he might arrange to rent the orchard house himself, and she meant to suggest this, though, at the same time, she found herself oddly reluctant to imagine anyone else there. She waited in growing impatience, then gave up at midnight, and was lighting another candle, ready to go upstairs, when the door was flung open and he stumbled in. Then she saw at once that their talk must wait. The feverish symptoms had set in again: the smell of drink was stronger, his speech blurred and enigmatic. He lurched towards her, muttering something she couldn't catch, waving his arms, knocking the candle from her hand - by accident, she thought, quickly treading on the flare. Suddenly he had pulled her down on to the couch, in a fierce grip that one couldn't mistake for an affable hug. Struggling to get away, still more surprised than frightened, she fought him off, managed to slide from his grasp, darted across the room and up the stairs, banging the door behind her. Halfway up she paused, listening to shuffling steps and curious shouts as he moved after her. Thankfully she remembered Dick's new bolt, and ran down to slide it across, realising - of course, Dick thought this might happen!

She sank down on the stair. A foot or so away, the door was pounded, shaken and kicked. The bolt held. There was a brief silence; more banging and yelling; another, longer silence; and then, far worse, an eerie wolfish scratching at the door panels. She crouched there, shivering: cross and frightened by turns, yet also shaken with giggles - that Derry, of all people, should be transformed into elderly wolf, drunken brawler, dangerous lecherous stranger.

Another silence: then a sound of something heavy slumping against the door, sliding to the ground ... and, after a long apprehensive wait, the snoring began again.

For her, sleep was out of the question. Upstairs she lay staring out at the moonlit trees, once more thinking with dread of the morning. Perhaps, as before, he might wake sober and pretend to remember nothing - but suppose he'd brought fresh supplies with him, and went on drinking and raving? She could be a prisoner, and no one would know. She thought of escape, of stealing out into the night, walking to Faro, taking the next train home; but her purse and other things were downstairs, and he must be lying so close to the door, the risk of waking him seemed too great.

She fell asleep at last in the early hours. And in the morning her problem had vanished: or Derry had. Venturing downstairs, she found with unspeakable relief that not only was he gone - he'd actually taken all his belongings with him.

So he must have realised that she'd had enough. No need to fear his coming back? No need, either, to change her plans and depart today. Setting the dishevelled room to rights, she thought that her fright had vanished as well, and looked forward to laughing with Sarah later about this weird adventure.

Then, as night fell, she began to feel less sure that he wouldn't be back. Too late, she wished she *had* left; now it seemed sheer folly to have let herself in for another night here alone. Indoors or out, there could be no pleasure. Twilight, moonrise, firelight, candlelight held none of the atmosphere she had hoped to enjoy for the last time.

Better pretend she *had* gone, that the house was deserted - so that, if he did come, he'd simply have to go away again. She locked the doors, blew out the candles, let the fire sink to ashes; and lay on the hearth, out of sight from the window, waiting with growing unease for the sounds she now felt all too sure of hearing.

At last they came: stealthy footfalls on the steps outside. A gleam of torchlight under the door. A knock; a pause, and another louder knock.

She told herself she had only to keep quiet ... and then, suddenly, sheer exasperation made her spring up and call -

"Oh, get out! Go away!"

There was another pause; and a cool voice said,

"Rowan, it's me. Do let me in."

Sarah's voice.

33

Sarah. As unexpected and welcome as a fairy godmother, and looking rather like one; wrapped in a long black cloak, leaning on a tall thumb-stick, a flashlight in her other hand.

"*Sarah*! Oh, am I glad to see you! Wait, I'll light the candles - "

"You do sound rattled. What's up?" Sarah flung off a knapsack, perched on the couch and gave Rowan a shrewd look. "Let me guess. Old Derry was more than you bargained for?"

"A lot more. How on earth did you know *that*?"

"I told Alex he'd moved in. We thought you might need rescuing."

"But - Sarah! - how did you get here? How did you find this place?" Her friend's arrival, so incredibly lucky and well-timed, began to seem mystifying.

She said with teasing calm, "Quite simple. Alex drove me down, Jamie brought me out from Faro - he couldn't stay, says he's got to chase up something."

"I know. She's called Melissa. His card says 'Far News. Ring Day or Night' ... only then they take the 'phone off."

"Anyway," Sarah added, "We knew you'd be all right *now*."

"Now you've come, yes. We'll have to get rid of Derry though - "

"Don't worry, you're rid already. He's been arrested."

"What!"

"Yes, it's true. This morning early."

"But - but - arrested! - whatever *for*?"

"Drunk driving, what else? Well, a good deal else, as a matter of fact. Did you know he's disqualified already? For years and years?"

"Oh God, of course I didn't. Nor did Jamie - "

"Then he crashed his car, the police found him - no one's hurt," she added quickly.

"But *when*? When was this?"

"Just this morning, I told you ... "

"But - he was here - he was asleep! He was drunk - "

"Yes, well ... he wasn't asleep at five a.m. or whenever it happened. Still too tight to drive straight of course. Crate of whisky on the back seat, too. So now he's in real trouble."

"But how did *you* hear?"

"He rang Jamie first thing, about bail. Trust Derry. And Jamie rang Alex."

"Oh ... He's out on bail?"

"Not yet he isn't. If ever. Alex said he'd try to fix it - and he's taking Derry back to London till his trial. So don't worry, you've lost your lodger. But - " Sarah hesitated, then went on slowly, "I came to ask - would you have *me* instead?"

"You! Oh yes, super - how long have you got?"

"Well, quite a long time. You're sure?"

"A long time? By yourself? I'm going back tomorrow - "

"You like it here, don't you? You keep saying so. Could we possibly stay on ... for the winter? Both of us?"

"For the *winter*!"

"Yes, Jamie wants you to, now he's lost Derry."

Rowan faltered, "I don't understand. What's happened?"

"Oh, this and that."

"You're ... feeling ill again?"

"Not ill, no. Not a bit. Not any more."

"Then - what *is* this? What about our jobs? What about Alex?"

"He's all for it. We were coming anyway, to ask you. You see - "
She stood up, shrugging off her cloak.

"I'm not Sarah just now. I'm Caro."

34

Another shock.

This time, staring at smiling pregnant Sarah, Rowan was speechless. At length she stammered - "'Caro'? What does that mean?" But already she began to guess.

"Caroline Harding. Mrs. Breck. It's all right - don't you see? - the baby's hers. Theirs. Going to be. It's all planned."

"Oh *Sarah* ... "

"No, Caro. You must remember. It's important."

She sat down again, watching Rowan pull herself together. Still dazed, Rowan turned away in silence, seeing to the fire, the candles, the kettle. She was thinking back, recalling things she hadn't understood at the time, now full of meaning. Her thoughts whirled: there was too much to say, to ask ... turning back, she brought out the most urgent question -

"*When?*"

"Mid-March. About St. Patrick's Day. I call her Paddy, I'm sure she's a girl."

"Oh. Oh yes."

"All right, you needn't start counting. I can tell her age to an hour, as someone said."

"And - Caro? She knows?"

"Of course not! She mustn't - not till the baby's here. That's why I need to come away."

"You mean she's never noticed? She's no idea?"

"She'd have said so like a shot, if she had. As a matter of fact - it's been quite easy. We haven't seen much of each other lately. She's out a lot in the evenings. That man she works for ... they go to concerts ... "

"And ... *Breck?*"

"Still stuck out there. With luck," she added airily, "he'll stay till spring and come home to a lovely surprise."

"You can't mean ... she'd let him think it's really hers!"

"She will if she takes my advice. Think how pleased he'll be. No need to spoil it."

"But that's not possible! She'd have told him the minute she knew ... wouldn't she?"

Sarah was silent for a moment. Then she said,

"Do you know - I don't believe she *could*. Too afraid of another let-down. No, I think she'd do exactly what I'm doing. Keep quiet as long as I can."

"But - but - what will she think you're up to, down here?"

"Like you. Helping Jamie. I said I could do with a change, and it was OK with Alex. So then I'll just stay on. With you."

"But you know I'm due back tomorrow - well, I *was* ..." Then Rowan cried, "Oh - then he knows. You've told Alex?"

"Oh, he guessed. Weeks ago. And he wanted to tell the father for me, he was sure he'd want us to get married. Isn't he a love? So I had to explain about Caro."

"Yes, but - " Rowan hesitated, then rushed on - "Sarah, what *about* him - the father? What about *him*!"

"Oh, she's got a good father. If she takes after him, she'll be all right."

Impossible not to run through the names, to wonder - *who?* Aware that Sarah was watching, reading her thoughts, Rowan fidgeted, picked up the coffee pot, then banged it down again:

"Listen. I didn't mean that, I mean - it'll be his too, won't it? He might want his child? Like Alex says, he might want to marry you?"

Sarah sat up abruptly, no longer smiling.

"*You* listen. I didn't cheat. (No thanks, I've gone off coffee.) 'God's honour', we used to say when we were kids ... He told me he couldn't stand infants, he'd never have one of his own. Once he went to see an ex-girl friend, married, with a new baby, and she looked ghastly, worn out, peeved as hell, and the poor brat kept yelling and throwing up, the place was foul, all smells and squalor. It put him off for life, he said."

Rowan was silent, thinking - yes, but he might change. He might grow up. You might manage better.

"So I asked him straight out. I said - suppose someone told you she was having your baby? And he said ... he said ... he'd find out exactly what his obligations were, and pay up ... and *that would be it*, he'd never go near either of them. Pretty definite, wouldn't you say?"

There was a faint tremor in Sarah's voice. Rowan said,

"That's all right, then. I just wondered."

And, she realised, it sounded all too likely. She remembered that angry barrister, long ago in the court tearoom. And something else, quite unforgettable, in a book of Rosamond Lehmann's: *He's not going to say, "Our child." He'll say, Christ, are you sure? What are you going to do?*

Sarah, lying back, suddenly looked wan and fagged. Rowan stopped arguing and took refuge in practical details: "Have you eaten? Can you still eat eggs? I'll get the fire going upstairs - you can sleep up there, some nurses left a wad of mattresses - oh!" she exclaimed with a flash of inspiration - "Listen, you can have the baby at Sheepskin House! It's a hospital, maternity wing - "

"I know. You told me, the first time you wrote."

So she had it all worked out. Coming here was no haphazard impulse. She'd thought of everything.

Or ... had she?

Treading more carefully now, Rowan warned herself - no more questions. Not till tomorrow anyway.

35

But tomorrow came more quickly than they knew. Both were far too excited to sleep yet. The talk went on for hours by firelight.

"Have you been to a doctor?"

"Yes, I found a woman in Norwich, I went there by bus. I did the Caro stuff, husband away ... it seemed to go down all right." She pointed to a narrow silver ring on her left hand. "I got this in a junk shop ..."

"So - when you book in at Sheepskin - will you tell *them* you're Caro?"

"Of course. Why not? I brought this ... " She rummaged in her pack and handed a card to Rowan: a national health medical card that said Caroline Harding. "That's me now. No one knows me here ... only Jamie, and he won't talk."

"And - they're going to believe you're twenty-four?"

"They won't have to. There - date of birth, 1937. I just altered it from 1931. Simple."

"Suppose Caro wants her card?"

"She'll find she's mislaid it. She'll get another. Everything's much easier than you think, if you *let* it be."

Everything?

"Sarah - it has to have a birth certificate, doesn't it?"

"*She*."

"Sorry ... and that shows the father's name? I saw mine, when I got my passport ... "

"So I'll give both their names. Breck and Caro. They *will* be her father and mother, you see." Sarah went on lightly, "After all - no one really knows who their father is. Do they? Only the mother knows, and not always her either. 'Really, Mr. Sibnorth!' - remember?"

Once in court a young barrister had asked a boy witness, "And the previous witness is your father?" - bringing this quip from his lordship, so that he'd blushed and rephrased the question, amid sympathetic grins from the learned friends.

" 'Lies of great men all remind us, We can make our lies sublime' ... Men make laws, women have to do the best they can. Do you know - my old cousin John in Norfolk says women have always given fancy ages, on marriage lines and census forms and everything, and got away with it ... Anyway," she added soberly, "think of Caro. She's what matters."

"Yes!"

"You know that evening she was crying - after Breck left? Because no luck again? That's when I decided."

"Yes ... I see."

"And I was lucky right away. And yet Caro ... queer, isn't it?"

"Mm."

"I thought I'd go and stay with John again, he's so wrapped up in all that research, he wouldn't care a bit, so long as one didn't give birth in his study. Only then you wrote about taking that woman to hospital, right on your doorstep! What a break - Alex thought so too - and it all fits in, doesn't it? Oh, and I've brought my savings book, I'll pay for my keep of course. Still - I know I'll be in your debt for ever - "

No you won't, Rowan amended silently. Quite the other way round.

This was true; though Sarah no doubt would have been astonished to hear it.

A few years earlier, Rowan had fallen into a private compulsive habit of assessing other people's looks; and always, in any gathering, she'd had to admit herself the plainest girl there. Then one day, when they were alone, Sarah had asked idly,

"That cousin of yours - Ralph - does he look like you?"

"Oh no, he's very good-looking."

"Do you mean you think you're not?"

"Well, I know I'm not."

And Sarah had returned, in the same casual tone, not politely at all - "What rot. Of course you are."

That was all. Afterwards, from a kind of superstitious dread - she *must* have been joking? - Rowan tried to forget about it. But an odd thing happened. Gradually, in those secret frank assessments, she imagined herself moving up a place or two. That was when the schoolboy notes began to arrive.

Jane Austen, as usual, had got it exactly right: after looking plain for fifteen years, to look 'almost pretty' gave one far more pleasure 'than a beauty from her cradle can ever receive.' And - but for Sarah - none of this might ever have happened.

So now she said quickly, "I often wished there was someone else here ... "

"But not randy old Derry? Made a pass, did he?"

"Sort of ... "

"Can't have been much fun?"

"Oh, a riot."

"Well, but - " Sarah was suddenly impatient - "Weren't *you* idiotic? Why have him here at all?"

"I know. I never meant to, he just moved in, I couldn't stop him. And he seemed so nice at first. Well, harmless. No way to get rid of him.. And it was only last night - "

"You know your trouble? You're too damn polite. Or dim or something. You have to learn to tell them to sod off ... don't laugh, I mean it." She paused, and added in a small voice,

"And you can tell me too, if you want to."

"You know I don't!"

But then, looking about her, seeing the place through Sarah's eyes - bare cold rooms, dim lights, melancholy autumn woods all round, and dark winter ahead - Rowan warned -

"Only - you do realise? - it's not like being at Caro's. More like camping out really - no bath even, you have to wash in the kitchen, with kettles, it's *freezing* ... oh, and Sarah - all right, yes, Caro - what on earth will you do all day?"

"Well - "

"And it's so *quiet*, you've no idea. And not working - on your own here, day after day - how long, four months? Five? - you'd be so bored, you'd go mad!"

Sarah stretched out lazily. She was smiling again.

"Shall I? Wait and see."

36

"I swear by Almighty God," the jury foreman threatened, "that I will diligently enquire and true presentment make of all such matters and things as are here given by me in charge on behalf of our Lady the Queen ..."

This was the resumed inquest on poor young Fred. The car driver, now accompanied by a solicitor, repeated his former account. The youth and his girl friend flatly contradicted it, each insisting that the car had taken the corner at speed on its wrong side, right in the path of the cyclist. They held to their story despite a great deal of innuendo - "Now tell us ... were you and the young lady *really* paying attention to passing traffic? Weren't you - shall we say - otherwise engaged at the time? And why did you not come forward at once to help? Were you - perhaps - somewhat in disarray?"

The wife did not appear. She had left home, the court was told, leaving no address.

The coroner told the jury that they must disregard anything but the sworn evidence heard today. The jury promptly returned a verdict of "Death due to dangerous driving." Afterwards Rowan asked Pip, "Will he be prosecuted, d'you think?"

"He might if the wife turns up to tell her tale. No address, indeed. How long before they start digging up the garden?"

She said despondently, "Do you know any married people who stay in love and nice to each other and all that?"

"Oh, scores. Look at our Golden Wedding corner ... not exactly a gripping read though, would you say?"

But at home Sarah pointed out - "Yes, we do know two. Breck and Caro."

Sarah had been back to pack trunks for herself and Rowan, and to secure Caro's approval of their sudden delightful plan to spend the winter together in Cornwall. She returned in a hired van with two tough young men who carried everything down from the road, parked Rowan's bicycle in the woodshed and shouldered Sarah's trunk up the stair. Single-minded as a mother cat, she took over the upper room. She had brought warm clothes - 'Chinese' tunic, baggy sweaters, conveniently fashionable - bedding, sheepskin slippers, a parcel of doll-sized garments ("a layette, it's called. Caro will want to choose all the rest of course") and another of knitting wool, with a booklet of instructions for the beginner; but so far this defeated them both. There was also a sack of books, the longest she could find: *Gone With The Wind, War and Peace, How Green Was My Valley, Middlemarch, The Small House At Allington*; and others, like *Madam Bovary*, that she'd never had time to try before. Now there would be time.

She settled in, tending her fire night and day; prowling about the woods, while Rowan was at work, gathering firewood in small cautious armfuls. Dick Monk came after church on Sunday to chop logs and kindling, and also fixed a stout rope hand-rail on the stair. He showed frankly his satisfaction at Rowan's having such a suitable companion, a young married friend whose husband was abroad.

Rowan's family, for their part, seemed surprisingly unsurprised by the change of plan; only insisting that they would still send her an allowance to be spent on 'proper meals.' Casual fireside snacks, coffee-shop breakfasts were out. Father's contribution, they agreed, must be honestly spent, though anything over might fairly go into Rowan's travel fund.

Having stopped feeling sick some time ago, Sarah now discovered a turn for cookery. She would lie down for an hour in the afternoons 'like an old lady,' then stroll up to the shop, where Mrs. Lilypot was full of homely advice and obstetrical memoirs. She also took a hand in their catering. So far, despite Dick's hints, they had put off tackling the kitchen range; but Sarah mastered the primus in one lesson, and dug out a tripod and griddle from a second-hand shop in Farmouth. Rowan was treated to cheap and nourishing surprises, laver bread, oatmeal griddle cakes, even black puddings, sliced thinly and fried to crisp wafers with eggs and potato scones: "forget about the blood and breadcrumbs or whatever, tell yourself it's quails and peacocks' tongues."

As the afternoons closed in Sarah found candles too dim to read by, and got Dick to buy a petrol lamp. Rowan came back one evening to find the room downstairs bathed in white light: like the Piccadilly Ladies, she commented, with a fleeting pang of regret for her candle-lit solitude. Sarah retorted,

"Go from me, girl, or I will sling you in the river."

"Oho. You've started *How Green* ..."

"There is catching it is, girl."

"I know. Takes everyone that way." By everyone she meant Ralph. There had been a school holiday when he'd talked only *Valley*-speak. At least, Lizzie had said, it made a change from Wold Grunter: the holiday before, he'd been deep in the Powys brothers.

Sarah's addiction took a practical form. That first evening, she had a cauldron of Welsh 'potch' simmering: potatoes blended with tomatoes, carrots and swedes into a thick peppery orange-coloured cream. On other nights there would be leek soup with ham in it, apple fool with ginger, herrings baked in a wrapping of green leek leaves, lemon peel and parsley.

Soon she was grumbling, "That book makes me ravenous, I'll get enormous far too soon." She switched to *Gone With The Wind*, then crooned in the tones of the deep South that that was even worse. It had led her to an American cook-book in Farmouth library, and to suppers of fried

119

chicken, hot 'biscuits', wild duck and chestnut   dressing, salads garnished with cream cheese and walnuts.

But Dr. Gordon at Farmouth said her weight was fine, and so was her progress. And a midwife who called to inspect 'the home facilities' took one look at the kitchen pump and primus, the wood fires and attic stair, then booked her a bed for March at Sheepskin House.

So far, as she'd predicted, all seemed to be plain sailing; and Rowan knew she must keep any doubts and fears to herself. Bridie, she hoped, would be an ally when the time came; but Bridie's next call was to say goodbye. She was moving back to the city hospital.

Peter Thoransen, astonishingly, had become a regular visitor. Meeting Sarah in the shop, he offered to supply them with vegetables from the Sheepskin garden, which he rented from the estate; and would bring a basket of mushrooms, chicory or red cabbage on his way to bell practice, or after the Sunday morning ringing. Rowan teased,

"You've certainly brought him on ..."

"Looking like this? Don't be witless. *Of course* he comes to see you."

"Not a hope. I never had a word before, hardly. (Only once, about this house.) Not many now, either."

"Don't you see - he can listen to me, and think about you. He watches you all the time, on the quiet."

"Anyway - all the girls must fancy him?"

"Oh they do, they do. You should hear Mrs. Lilypot. Not a chance though. Keeps to himself. Brooding, she calls it."

"All the better to make an impression?"

"No. She thinks ... he's never got over the war. Doesn't care for the English much. We had such an easy time."

"Oh? London? Coventry? Plymouth?"

"Yes, yes. But ... we weren't *occupied*."

And his parents died, she remembered.

"I'll tell you a funny thing," Sarah mused. "He's afraid of you somehow. As if ... oh, as if you might know something against him. He comes to see if you've found out yet. I do wonder *what*?"

"Oh, really! Are you getting fey - out here all on your own with nature? Better come in sometimes and help me with the 'phoning."

"All right. But - " Sarah promised - "I'm not wrong."

120

37

Winter set in with a week of storms. Day and night a south-westerly gale filled the valley with salt spray and tore the leaves off the trees, while drenching rain stirred the river shallows and swamped the little waterfall. At night Rowan moved upstairs for company, and they lay awake listening to the uproar; yet with no sense of danger, for the house stood firm as a rock in its sheltered niche. If it weren't for the poor sailors, they agreed, these wild nights would simply have seemed exciting.

For Sarah the days were another matter. Her freedom curtailed by the weather, she spent long hours alone in a grey-green twilight that gave way to early darkness. Rain came in squalls, drumming on the roof, then dying away into silence. She began to find the quiet spells almost sinister, and caught herself straining to listen for curious sounds from outside. At nightfall, for instance, there would be a slight rasp like animal claws on the steps, then a faint shuffling close to the door, and a snorting or snuffling under it. Not a dog, she thought; and not the donkey, Peregrine, who knew how to tap for admission with a hoof.

Why not open the door and look? But she felt a primitive reluctance to let the wild dark into her safe bright cave. As she hesitated, there would come padding sounds of retreat; and silence again. Sometimes too she fancied something more unnerving: a small white face at the window, glimpsed for a moment, then vanishing.

When Rowan came back, none of that seemed worth mentioning. But one morning, lugging her bicycle to the path, Rowan called,

"Sarah - Caro! Come and look - there's been a badger!"

A paw-mark on a molehill; another on the steps, imprinted on a smear of mud, like fork marks on mashed potato.

"Perhaps he used to get food here - we could put something out for him?" She began to tell Sarah about the badger prints on the shore, never yet revisited. "I meant to send photos to Lizzie ... and Ralph ... We could go there next Sunday, shall we, if it's fine?"

Halfway up the slope she called back, "Cheese or an apple or something -"

"What?"

"For the badger - don't forget?"

Sarah did forget until darkness fell: then opened the door a crack, flung out a lump of cheese, shut and locked hurriedly ... and turned to catch another presence at the window, flashing eyes, flying hair: a ghostly child, wearing glasses? Nothing there now.

She gave the dark panes a thoughtful survey, and went upstairs to write a letter, asking Caro if those old velvet curtains were still in her attic cupboard, and could they be lent to the orchard house?

The storms died away, and Sunday brought a pale quiet morning for their walk to the sea. Setting out along the river path, they saw that the season was changed, the spirit of autumn lost. Golden woods, summer flowers and insects were only a memory; birds, but for one resonant thrush, made small moping sounds. The stream ran sullenly, choked with leaves; the beeches were bare, and new red-brown buds gleamed in the wintry light.

Sarah, they decided, had better not risk the steep slide from the cliff-top. Instead they crossed the dunes and open sands and make their way around the curving reef into the horseshoe cove, patterned as before by prints of night-wandering badgers. The cave had a curious iron grating like a portcullis, set high in the rock above the entrance. Inside it narrowed from a wide chamber to a dark tunnel, smelling of old bananas that someone had left there. The badger tracks led inward along the tunnel until they disappeared through a narrow gap in the wall: the entry perhaps to a sett up there in the cliff.

Nearing home again, they found more prints on the pathway, a burrow opening under an ash clump near by, and close to that a half-buried log, skinned and deeply scored by raking claws: no doubt the domain of their evening visitor. Sarah now heard him come and go without a tremor. Nor was she troubled by faces, real or illusory, at the window. Before dark she would draw the long curtains sent by Caro. Their faded rose-red folds, shutting out the night, were a comfortable reminder of a bedroom shared in childhood.

Indoor fauna - woodlice, centipedes, spiders, a wintering slow-worm in the privy - she still found trying; but she had grown fond of the cricket's chirp, and of the tiny fawn-coloured moths that came out at night to flap around the lamp and risk death in bedside candles. She even looked in the Farmouth library for a book on moths, but found only a slim text-book for children, *Collecting Butterflies and Moths.*

This lacked the coloured plates and lists of names she had in mind, but proved rewarding. The author hoped, he wrote, to introduce young naturalists to a fascinating hobby; and he gave instructions on the catching, killing and setting of 'specimens'. But some young readers had more up-to-date ideas, and one of them had added heartfelt footnotes:

Don't take any notice of this wicked ~~man~~ boy let the little moths ~~live~~ die – you just /do not watch them: please do ~~not~~ kill them. ~~How~~ They would ~~he~~ like to be killed just for "fun". He is ~~a/~~ not a very wicked man, children do not believe.

Inevitably, a mischief-maker had joined in with subversive corrections – resulting in a contest –

YES

WICKED
MAN!

while on another page a third hand added:

Do /^{not} kill who write in the book because I think what he or she said was very right every word of it

    Something else to tell Ralph, Rowan thought, when I write to him.

    Her photographs of the badger prints on the shore had been a success, and she wrote a long letter to send with them. But then doubt set in, and she burned it to ashes, like an unlucky moth, in her candle.

38

One morning in December Sarah was in the Far News office, helping Rowan to deal with the post, when she found a letter addressed to herself and sent on by Caro. A Christmas card, with a plaintive message from one of her men: "Where in the world have you got to?"

Christmas. They looked at one another and agreed, with a shrug of dismissal - nothing to do with us. We're too old for Christmas.

All this month there had been signs of preparation. Jamie and Rowan, with a local cameraman, were supplying rural items for a Christmas Eve feature in a London paper - rehearsals for bell-ringing, carolling, a children's Nativity play; also tree-lifting and mistletoe cutting. The plantation in the water woods had been stripped of its Christmas trees by men from Woods Farm. In Sheepskin park the lime grove had lost its leaves, disclosing dark clumps of mistletoe to be cut with long-handled shears, the pickers wading through drifts of blond leafage that matched the coats of fallow deer sheltering there from the wind. Ivy trails in the woods were splashed with red and yellow, as though for decoration; pink spindle-berries had split to show tiny bright seed pearls, and the holly tree flaunted its green and scarlet. *The berries redden up to Christmas time ...* but that message had its counterpoint: *What's Christmas time unless there be Some other in the house than we?*

The time of gifts was for children. Next year, or the year after, all that could begin again for Breck and Caro and Aunt Sarah. This was a quiet waiting time: *The fallow fawns invisible go, With the fallow doe* - invisible, like Sarah's child, because not yet born.

Their families were warned not to expect them home, and took the news calmly. Rowan posted a card to Aunt Lizard, hoping to have a reply at last to her question about the picture; which Lizzie, preoccupied no doubt with Rufus, had so far overlooked. Dick Monk promised to find them a brace of pheasants, in tones which ruled out any refusal, and Mrs.Lilypot with equal firmness sold them a pudding and a jar of mincemeat. But that would be all: no other special food, no boring decorations. Just an ordinary weekend.

But suddenly, with three days to go, everything changed.

Coming back from an early walk to the shop, they found strangers in the orchard, a young woman and a little girl: but strangers only for a moment, before mutual recognition. The woman was Lesley Black, one of Lizzie's pupils in her art-teaching days, now living with her daughter Tabby in Lizzie's Chelsea studio. They had come down on the night train, hoping to stay at the inn. Lesley was doing illustrations for a children's book, and she wanted to make sketches of the orchard house, the folly, the stone faun and lion seat.

Over breakfast she explained, "We had this house, Tabby and I, when she was a baby ... how did *you* come here?"

When Rowan got from Arran Green to the lawyer's letter, she laughed. "What! Not old Hand and Glove? At Lincoln's Inn? They wrote to me too."

"Oh ... then who did it belong to, when you came?"

"Do you know ... no one ever actually told me. They said it was a friend, and we could live here rent free, as long as we liked -"

"Yes. That's what they told me!"

" - so I guessed it must be Tabby's grandmother. Mrs. Falconer. She wasn't a friend exactly, but - Denys and I had just broken up - she knew I'd nowhere to go - and I thought I must accept, because of the baby. And it's lovely here, isn't it? We were awfully happy ..."

Another bit of the past, Rowan thought. The gamekeepers, the Thoransens, wartime refugees perhaps, then Lesley: and Arran Green must have bought the house at some time after that?

Lesley went on, "Look, I've got to go and work, thanks for breakfast -"

"But we'll see you again? Where are you staying?"

"Not sure yet. I used to know the people at the inn - but they're gone. Sure to be a guest house open in St. Max ..."

"Two or three," Rowan agreed, "and you're not going to any of them. *Of course* you must stay with us."

The luck was two-fold, they found: a child for Christmas, and an ally who knew the house well, took the camping element for granted - Lesley and Tabby had sleeping-bags, and would curl down happily on spare mattresses upstairs - and who brought the deft touch of experience to their novice housekeeping.

The daunting kitchen range - ignored so far, despite all Dick's hints - held no terrors for Lesley. She fiddled confidently with lids, flaps and levers, lit and relit the fire, coaxed and cursed it by turns while it smoked, sulked and raised false hopes only to damp them again; until it relented and settled down to burn steadily, the top rings glowing, the heavy kettle humming, and the oven in due course sending out festive smells of cake and pastry.

Apples and jacket potatoes were no longer scorched in the hot wood-ashes but cleanly baked in the old bread oven, a warm tunnel hidden behind a little iron door in the fireplace wall; and a crock of oatmeal, set in there overnight, would turn itself into breakfast porridge, with no crusted sooty pan for the washer-up.

Also Lesley knew how to skin a rabbit, pluck pheasants, peel chestnuts, make mince pies and pasties and delectable bread sauce; yet somehow contriving to do all this with the air of a diffident guest merely offering to lend a hand here and there.

These enterprises filled the evenings; by daylight they went their separate ways to work. Meanwhile the silent child haunted the woods at all hours, came in to tea looking rapt and bemused, then vanished again into the winter twilight. Indoors, by looks more often than words, she showed implicit trust in her hosts - Where shall we hang our stockings? When can we fetch the Tree? - and pleasure in their arrangements: Could I work the pump myself? Is it time to feed the badger?

Wouldn't she feel lonely, playing outside by herself, Rowan asked. But her mother said,

"She's in heaven, she loves the country. Only now I wish we'd brought her cat, she misses him so much ..."

39

On their second morning Rowan cycled out to the fields to write a caption for a picture of flower-pickers. She was dubious about this errand, and relieved to find a crew of decorative young women happy to pose with armfuls of daffodils, while Mrs. Monk stayed aloof and scowling in the background. The daffodils had been picked in bud and brought into flower in a greenhouse. But - "Why waste two days?" Rowan asked the old packer. "Why not sell them in bud?" He gave her a pitying look.

That evening at home she found a gala scene. Sarah and Tabby had filled the house with greenery, lighted tall silver candles and decked out a tree with strings of rose-hips, little scarlet crab apples and snow-berries, gilded cones, garlands of old-man's-beard sprayed with frost, miniature tapers and crackers. It gleamed in the shadows at the far end of the room, and over tea Lesley told them,

"You know - I remember my *first* Christmas tree. At a village school, in the Infants ... I'd only just started, and it was all a bit chaotic, 'Now-children-all-together', the Ten Commandments and the Beatitudes and the ABC and 'The Three Bears' ... and suddenly all that stopped, and the room was dark and quiet, the last afternoon of term - and there was this lovely shining thing, and a present for everyone. Dolls for the girls, in woolly shifts, and guess who'd done all that knitting? The six-year-olds in the top class! I was struggling with my first string dish-cloth, and there were those tots plain-and-purling away like little old grannies - socks for their brothers too."

"Didn't the boys learn?"

"Heavens no, *they* did drawing and modelling, and on the tree they had packs of Glitterwax, gorgeous stuff, I longed for that instead of a doll."

Rowan exclaimed, "Sarah - Caro - did you hear? Lesley can knit! Come on, do show us -"

"Oh well ... that was a lifetime ago. I didn't knit for Tabby, no time, it was book jackets not matinée coats (why matinée one wonders?) All right, we can try if you like."

"There's a book of directions, that might help?"

But, as the girls already knew, the booklet had been written by an expert with no idea how to teach the ignorant. Arguing over the diagrams, deriding each other's efforts, they were too preoccupied to notice when Tabby slipped back in from her twilight prowl, took up a pair of needles, cast on a row of stitches and began to knit. Then it was - "Tabby, you're a marvel. Could you teach us - as a Christmas present?"

Late in the evening, when the marvel was asleep, Lesley brought down a bag of small objects to wrap for her stocking. After a few minutes she said casually,

"Do tell me. Why is Caro sometimes Sarah?"

Dead silence made her look up. The pair, sorting indoor fireworks on the table, stared dumbly at her. Rowan looked guilty, her friend taken aback; until she laughed and decided - "I suppose we could tell *you*." And did so, in two sentences.

It was Lesley's turn to be startled. At length she said slowly,

"I see. Poor Caro. That old problem ..."

"*Is* it old? She says it's horribly up to date, they're doing a lot of research."

"Yes. Still ... it keeps cropping up, doesn't it? In the Bible, I seem to remember? And folklore? Two or three stories in here, actually ..." She was wrapping *The Gold Fairy Book*. "One where the queen hasn't any children, so when the king's away she adopts a peasant baby, then she sends someone to tell him they've got a son."

"And does he - ?"

"Oh yes, he believes her. Or says he does. I suppose he wants to - that's rather the point, isn't it?"

Another silence. Lesley went on carefully,

"I mean - I don't think you're doing anything unheard of. Lots of precedents, aren't there? The baby in the warming-pan, and so on ..."

"I said that!" Sarah broke in. "Didn't I, Rowan? And I said Breck will go along with us - even if he knows it was me."

"And then they might have one of their own as well - people sometimes do, after they adopt?"

"Yes, and," Sarah told her, "Caro's only twenty-four, time enough - think of Lizzie, not marrying till now!"

Rowan suddenly remembered - "She was married before, though - quite young, she must have been -"

"I never knew that?"

"Yes, a girl in Ireland told me. She was Mrs. Ransome or Transom or something ... I suppose he died."

"No children?"

"Of course not - we'd have known them, wouldn't we? Then she and Rollo were lovers for years, can't think why they didn't marry sooner -" Rowan stopped short, aware that the same might be said of Lesley and her friend Guy.

"People change," Lesley offered. "When we parted I felt so lost, I thought I'd marry the first man who asked me. Only, when someone kindly did, I found I couldn't -" risk losing another home, she'd nearly said. All too easy to find oneself deluded. Like a spider taking over a Sunday teapot ...

But one shouldn't bore the young with such stuff. Anyway, they wouldn't believe it, and quite right too. She began to collect her packages.

"Coming, Sarah Caro? Christmas Eve tomorrow. Of all the days in the year."

40

Tomorrow brought a rush of preparation, plucking, skinning, chopping, slicing, in a cloud of pungent smells - singed feathers, rabbit and bacon frying, herbs and onions, celery and apples, orange salad, spice and cloves and lemon peel. Dick Monk brought a chicken from Sheepskin Farm to eke out the pheasants. Rowan calculated anxiously, "That should be enough now, don't you think? Even if Guy comes?"

"Oh yes, he's coming. He'll be here to breakfast."

Then Sarah, back from the shop, produced a bag of artichokes, seakale and endive.

"Peter sent this. And look," she added nervously, "I asked him to dinner tomorrow ..."

Rowan laughed. "Optimist! As if he would." Then, seeing Sarah's expression - "You don't mean he's coming!"

"Well yes, he is. Will that be all right?" They both turned to Lesley, who assured them, "Fine."

"Yes, but wait - he said he'll bring a duck to roast -"

A slight pause. Then -" So long as he brings it in good time."

"Oh, he's going to. When they ring for early service." Sarah added with relief, "I was afraid you'd feel like Mrs. Cratchit. You know - when Scrooge sends that ghastly turkey at the last minute."

As the bells of St. Max church pealed out at daybreak Guy sauntered in, hung with baggage, keyed up from his long night drive over empty starlit roads; setting down a guitar, a pack full of presents, crackers, flowers, a ham, a pineapple, gold-topped bottles; a second pack, holding borrowed glasses; and then, with infinite care, another offering: Tabby's dear cat Tray, flat-eared but resigned, safe in a lidded basket. "Just what I wanted" would never have been more heartfelt.

Hours later, just before sunset, Rowan slipped out of doors into the chill pine-scented silence of the wild garden. Tabby came after her with the cat on a long lead, running ahead and up the slope, where Tray began to frolic in demented circles, acknowledging no restraint.

The little thorn tree by the bridge now held a holly wreath and two new trinkets, cracker toys perhaps, a ring and a tiny medallion shaped like a cat's face. Could Tabby have put them there? It was on the tip of her tongue to ask; but child and cat were intent on their game, and she strolled on through the trees to sit on a wooden seat at the top of the wilderness. Tabby joined her presently, and they perched together while Tray frisked about, winding and unwinding his lead around a great tree-trunk.

The wilderness lay hushed in the peace and stillness of Christmas afternoon. To a world where mighty dread was never absent, the day had brought back its ancient truce. In the low brilliant light the grass was vivid emerald; cedars, pines and spruces glowed like Christmas trees. Lights shone from an upper window in Sheepskin House, and Rowan said idly,

"I wonder if there's been a baby today."

"Yes. Two. Twins."

She hadn't expected any response; least of all this shy assurance. Could Tabby be romancing?

"Really? How do you know?"

"*She* told me. Linky."

"Who ... who is Linky?"

A look of surprise. "Their sister. One of them."

One of them. One of *them*.

She stared at Tabby, and it dawned on her ... she hadn't been lonely, or alone. For her, the watchers must have come out of hiding. Unable somehow to question this secretive little creature, Rowan looked away again; and found herself observing a distant figure down on the riverside path, passing the orchard, coming uphill at a brisk pace. A woman, smartly dressed, carrying daffodils, making for the hospital perhaps? Humming and smiling to herself, she went by without seeing them. The door into the walled garden creaked open and shut; and Rowan said aloud in sheer amazement,

"My goodness - that was Mrs. Monk!"

"M'hm."

"You know *her* too? What's happened ...! I never thought she could look like that!"

Tray pounced on a dead leaf, jerking the lead out of Tabby's hand, springing away. Jumping after him, Tabby said something over her shoulder. Rowan called -

"What? Didn't hear you -"

"I said ... someone sent her a Christmas card."

Rowan was going to retort - "Is that all!" But at once she realised: it depends *who*.

All through this week she hadn't been able to help snatching up the office post, glancing through quickly, wondering, not exactly hoping. No use to think defensively, men don't send cards. Some did. Only the one she wished for hadn't come.

In the distance the garden door creaked again, and footsteps brushed the grass behind a belt of laurels. Someone spoke to Tabby.

Peter's voice.

He'd gone out earlier to check the glasshouses. She sat very still, and felt herself begin to shiver. Would he see her in passing? Would he stop?

He wasn't, as they'd rather feared, proving a difficult guest. After a glass or two he seemed friendly and relaxed, at ease with Guy, pleased to see Lesley again: in the past, when short of money, she had worked with his flower-pickers.   To Rowan herself he'd barely spoken; yet, primed by Sarah's remarks, she seemed to feel his awareness.

The footsteps drew near, and came to a halt. He moved across to stand in front of her. Looking up, she waited for him to speak; but he said nothing at all.

They remained looking gravely at each other, as though in mutual questioning. His hair was bright against the dusky laurels. His face had the cold impersonal beauty of the stone Antinous. A face out of a ballad: *You'll get no kiss of that comely mouth, Though you should break your heart ...*

Then he was beside her, their arms about each other. He was talking in low tones, saying the same words over and over, foreign words, unknown yet familiar, caressing: unmistakable words of love. The shock and delight were overwhelming, she couldn't respond in speech, but only with her touching hands. The light faded, and they sat on in chill twilight that seemed radiant as a summer evening. She felt as though she'd been given a longed-for message: not the one she had waited for, yet immeasurably comforting.

He stirred at last, not releasing her but raising his head a little. Now she sensed that he was smiling, opened her eyes, and saw what he had seen: two small green lights glinting in shadow a yard or two away. Cat's eyes.

Tabby hovered there, clasping Tray, tense with some urgent plea or expectation, waiting patiently for their notice. She whispered -

"Please...Is it dark enough *now?*"

"?"

"To light our Tree?"

It was near midnight when Peter set out for home, striding away by torchlight down the river path. They all stood out on the steps, watching the faint beam until it was lost in the woods.

The church clock struck twelve. Then, far off, they heard him begin to whistle: *It came upon the midnight clear ...* The high notes rang out, and faded in turn, leaving only the sound of wind-blown trees and water.

Christmas was over. In a few hours the others would be gone.

What will happen to us all, Rowan wondered, before we hear Christmas music again?

The warmth and wild happiness of the evening lasted hour after hour through a feverish night, until she drowsed off, to wake in panic, starting up, thinking - what possessed me? All these *years* I've been in love with Ralph, I'm going out there to find him. How could I make such a fool of myself? I don't care a scrap for anyone else, of course I don't ...

Daylight, as daylight does, brought a calmer view. Thankfully she realised - it was just the champagne, and the day, and so on - everyone knows about Christmas parties! The same for him, thank goodness - no need to make a thing of it.

But, when he appeared later that morning, the champagne theory vanished. Their looks met with the same pulse of hidden excitement they had shared the night before; something far beyond pastime or flirtation.

And then, before she could begin to sort out her feelings, to distinguish between delight and disquiet, hope and fear - the episode was over; snuffed out like a candle, somehow, by a short and quite irrelevant exchange.

Lesley, coming downstairs, ready to leave, called to Rowan -

"When is it you're going?"

"Well ..." Reluctant, from superstition, to commit herself to dates, Rowan told her, "Not long now."

"I wonder - could you take some stuff for Lizzie? Brushes and things? And a mug for Rufus?"

In the flurry of their departure, she lost sight of Peter for a few moments. Then, looking back from the doorway, she saw that he was still standing where she'd last seen him. Again their eyes met, and now she saw something had changed between them. He had gone very white; she thought he looked stricken, almost ill.. Meeting her gaze, he crossed to her side, saying with his old abruptness - "You're going away?"

And, as she didn't speak -

"To New Zealand? To the aunt?" His tone was almost accusing. "*Soon?*"

She nodded, still trying to find words, to ask - *what is it? What's the matter?*

He simply shrugged in response; a bleak despairing gesture that said plainly - That's it, then. Finis. Springing down the steps, sketching a wave for the others, he vanished over the bridge and out of her life.

---oOo---

III

Sheskin the music of your name and your waters

*

Sheskin, O Sheskin, all the things that are Sheskin,

*

Please be there, and let me be there to come back.

T.H. White: *Sheskin*

41

The long dark evenings were what she'd once dreaded for Sarah; needlessly, as she now realised. Her friend never seemed at a loss for amusement. This month, as it happened, she was deep in the affairs of a local group, the Farmouth Players, and recounted it all to Rowan as they lounged at night by the fire, eating boiled eggs or toasted kippers. Fireside picnics were back again: she had no time at present for experimental cookery.

The Players were rehearsing "Romeo and Juliet" for a regional Shakespeare contest; the winners to give scenes from their production at a London theatre. In Farmouth coffee-shop Sarah had fallen into talk with the producer, Bob Lawson, a stage-struck schoolmaster, and two bright occidental stars, Don Dennison and his sister Delia, disconsolately playing Juliet's parents.

"Of course they'd have jumped at R and J if Bob had let them. Guess what, though? - he was mad keen to get Peter for Romeo!"

"*Oh ...*"

"Yes, wouldn't he look terrific? Not a chance of course. He said he'd never done any acting -"

("Not true. What about our charades?"

"Only because Tabby picked him) - and Bob said all the better, he could learn, he'd bring such freshness etcetera ... only Peter just laughed."

"So who -?"

"Oh, it's mostly new members, kids from the grammar school. Bob did Hamlet there last year, with proper fencing lessons, so now Ophelia's Juliet, and Hamlet and Laertes and the understudies are Romeo and all the chaps, killing each other off in style - how are they still alive till now, one might ask?"

"They're all just back from different Wittenbergs?"

Sarah had quickly been recruited to produce spare copies of the parts on Rowan's new typewriter, bought with a Christmas cheque from Ireland; then to watch rehearsals and act as prompter, since she knew the text already from their own sixth form days ... "Only," she told Rowan, "I don't seem to care for this play really, now I see such a lot of it. The second half anyway, where it gets so dismal and stupid. I mean - if the Friar's going to pack her off with Romeo when she wakes up - why not do that in the first place? Why all the gloom and misery, and that idiotic caper in the vault?"

"We know why. Anyway, once you start carping - everything's pretty far-fetched, don't you think? Look at old Capulet, all fatherly one minute, 'my child is yet a stranger in the world,' and next it's 'Hang thee young baggage,' go out and starve, and so on ..."

"No, fair enough, that's just like all fathers. The real oddity's that wicked Nurse I think ... egging her on with Romeo, then trying to marry her off again to Paris -*why*?"

"Oh, because she may be pregnant, and think what a row there'll be, Nurse will be in dead trouble -"

"She would be anyway, wouldn't she, if the parents knew what she was up to? The old twister - "

"Yes, but - suppose she's really Juliet's mother? Like 'Lady Clare' you know - the baby died, and she put her Susan in its place? So she's madly jealous, she wants to run Susan's life."

"H'm. I never thought of that!"

"I bet some learned don has."

"Anyway," Sarah added, "Our Nurse is going to be good, a nice bawdy old thing, a change from the blooming sixth-formers. Only the other regulars are fed up - Delia keeps quoting 'You can't play Juliet till you're forty,' and Friar Lawrence wanted Mercutio, imagine, and Don goes on about Leslie Howard, forty at least, in that film we saw ... look, we're doing another run-through on Sunday, come and watch?"

This proved more diverting than they could have foreseen. They arrived to find the rehearsal abandoned and an argument in progress, developing rapidly into a blazing row of almost Montagu-Capulet bitterness.

Discontent with Bob Lawson's casting, already smouldering for weeks, had erupted into open rebellion, led by the two Dennisons. By the end of the morning Farmouth had two dramatic societies and two separate competition entrants: the Players, left in possession of the hall, and Bob's newly-styled Young Stagers, who departed, on a wave of hilarity, to recruit fresh talent at school and press on to hopes of victory.

Sarah, invited by both to remain as prompter, withdrew tactfully to spend the afternoon with Rowan in the Far News office, helping to touch up this rural drama for the morning papers. On a quiet Sunday, the 'crabbèd age and youth' angle appealed to one or two gossip editors, and next day the rivals found themselves enjoying a moment of fame, spiced with flattery for the gallant young and mild ridicule for their seniors, who carried it off with disdain. Later, on judgement day, one paper revived the story, with pictures of the rival lovers, unkindly contrasted, to the artless glee of the school party.

To suit the adjudicator, a tutor from a London drama academy, both performances were given on a Saturday afternoon, the Young Stagers drawing first place. Their version went well, and afterwards the judge's remarks were indulgent enough to raise high hopes. Bubbling with excitement, they piled into the hall with their friends to join the audience for the Players' turn. Only Bob Lawson felt unequal to this. Exhausted by weeks of rehearsing, he escaped for a quiet prowl in the dusk; a mistake he would greatly regret.

Trouble showed signs of brewing almost at once, when faint ironic cheers from the young greeted a cautious duel between Tybalt and Benvolio. Next, Romeo's love-sick speeches brought a few titters, quickly hushed. There was no malice in this, only childish levity; but the fatal spark of mockery was lit, setting off fits of muffled laughter that could hardly be long hidden. Bob Lawson could have checked them, but he was far out of earshot in the bar of the Ship. Soon the lines about Juliet's age, unwisely uncut, produced such riotous giggles that the play was halted, the lights turned on, and the society's chairman stood up with heated demands for fair play and good manners. The joke was over. The culprits subsided or slipped away, and the Players were left to carry on as best they could.

And now these angry veterans showed their mettle. The 'best they could' proved far beyond anything seen at rehearsals. Scene after scene took on a defiant pace and verve; so that Sarah in the prompt corner found herself with nothing to do (no question now of any fluffing or faltering) but watch a transformation - ardent lovers, sprightly Mercutio, dashing Tybalt, and the dire advance of tragedy that, for the first time, left her close to tears as the curtain fell and the adjudicator rose to begin his comments with high praise for their professionalism.

Some weeks must pass before the contest winners would be named. In Farmouth, however, the real contest was felt to be over, and the Players, with a sense of moral victory, turned to plans for their next production.

But perhaps there were still secret hopes. Miss Pichegru, the wardrobe mistress, confided to Sarah,

"When those brats were sniggering at Delia I just couldn't stay and listen. I got out and I went across to the church ... and *I lit a candle for St. Jude.*"

"Oh? Patron saint of actors?"

"Well, my dear, no. Lost causes."

42

Rowan's coming to the orchard house, once so lightly accounted for, had acquired an air of mystery since the talk at Christmas. If, as seemed logical, the house had passed from one owner to another - from Tabby's grandmother to Arran Green - there were still such quirks of coincidence as to make this curious.

So why not write to Arran Green and ask straight out if he had sent her?

But the time for that was past, she found; somehow the letter wouldn't get itself written. And soon her thoughts were taken up with a more pressing matter. Derry Gillespie was to appear before Faro magistrates, accused of 'drunk driving', driving while disqualified and driving a defective car.

When the day arrived, she begged Jamie - "Would *you* do it? I don't want to sit there and hear him sent for trial" - or worse, she feared: tried on the spot, and sent down.

"Not to worry. They'll put him in one of those holiday camps, he'll be the life and soul."

But this had a hollow ring. He amended seriously,

"Everyone's rallied round, he'll have first class counsel."

To say *what*, she wondered. Could any excuses be offered on such grave charges? And afterwards she heard without surprise that he had pleaded guilty to everything. He was remanded for sentence to the Quarter Sessions in March.

Yet, after all, counsel *had* found something to say on his behalf. The court was told that, after losing his driving licence, Derry had set out to find a new career in the west country, making a brave attempt to give up drinking and to do without a car; and had lapsed only because in fact he was gravely ill and often in great pain. He would now await sentence in hospital.

"Jamie! Did he ever tell you ...?"

"Not a word. Poor chap. Looks pretty seedy, I must say. But who wouldn't, in his shoes?"

"You don't think ... they might be shooting a line?"

"H'm. Quite an affecting one, if so. Clever old Arran Green - Alex thought he'd do a good job if anyone could."

"Arran Green - no! It was *him*? Oh, I must see him -"

A flying search of the court and car park proved useless. By now he might be well on the way to Exeter. Where else to look? There would be a London train at noon. She raced across, scanned the platform, and saw him at once in the distance.

An odd figure, she thought, in this alien setting: impressive, almost theatrical-looking, in dark cloak and wide-brimmed hat.

He was not alone. A girl waited at his side - a pupil in his chambers, seen once or twice in court last autumn - her face upturned as she listened, intent and deferential, to the well-remembered voice. The train was already signalled; there was no time to lose if Rowan were to present herself, break into his monologue, and somehow contrive to ask him about the orchard house ...

She drew near, and his glance travelled over her absently. He stood back a pace or two to let her pass, and she realised - *he doesn't remember me yet*! She paused for a moment, at a loss, then pressed forward. When she spoke he gazed blankly, arrested in mid-period, before recognition dawned:

"Rowena! Isn't it - ?"

"Rowan ..."

"Indeed yes. But what a charming surprise! My dear child - whatever brings *you* to Faro?"

Her last glimpse showed them seated in the luncheon car, sunlight flashing on cutlery as the train drew out of the shadowed station. He turned to pull down a shade for his companion, glanced through the window, smiled and waved in kindly farewell.

Watching them out of sight - that final, fated act - she laughed inwardly, recalling, "Women! You have to feed them and fuss over them ..." And she knew, without a trace of doubt, that there'd been no need for her unspoken question. Arran Green had had no part whatever in sending her to Sheepskin.

43

"Curiouser and curiouser. To coin a phrase." Sarah looked up from the cot quilt she was knitting: a suitably aunt-like present, they'd agreed. "So - what made you think it was *him* to start with?"

"Well, he did seem quite concerned. But I suppose that's just his way." No doubt he was now dealing out shrewd advice to her successor; besides harrowing her with his own life history.

"He was right too, wasn't he? The country does suit you."

"I know. But - " not yet, she thought with secret fear; not for ever. Now was the time to see men and cities. Christchurch next. Even at the risk of finding that she'd left her heart in Cornwall.

"And you've never met that Mrs. Thing - Tabby's grandma?" Sarah pursued. "So who does own the house? Someone must know. I'll do a bit of probing, shall I?"

But this brought no result. She found that Mrs.Lilypot, so well informed in other directions, had known the house only since the phase of the nurses' parties; having come to St. Max a couple of years ago to help her father-in-law with the shop when his wife died. Dick Monk, of course, had evaded all enquiries from the start; as though, like the lawyers, he'd promised secrecy. And his brother Bert Monk proved equally unhelpful. Appearing in the yard one day with a sack of coal for the bin, he fobbed off any question of payment with Dick's formula - " all seen to ... agents ... upkeep" - while he glared at her from his one good eye that, with a black eye patch and gruff accents, lent him a fierce piratical air.

The same odd sense of concealment seemed to overhang another topic: the badgers in the woods and the cove. More than once, buying stale currant buns or extra cheese for their night visitor, Sarah had spoken of him and of the paw-prints on the shore; but these remarks appeared to go unheard. Mrs. Lilypot would simply change the subject, and Dick Monk too made no response.

It was Jamie who discovered why that subject was taboo. A policeman told him that the badger colonies were raided from time to time by men from far-away towns, hoping to trap the creatures in nets and sell them to badger-baiting clubs. Sometimes the marauders would get away with their prey; and sometimes not. Either way, the natives felt, the less said the better.

One Sunday morning Sarah and Rowan set out to revisit the cove. Recalling a tale of Mrs. Lilypot's about a short cut to the sea, they began by climbing up into the folly and making their way to a grotto behind it; a dim cavern, lit by a glass panel in the roof, where a figure in a marble robe reclined beside a pool, wearing a spiky crown and a sinister smile. Another archway led on to a tunnel, sloping away into darkness. They had brought torches to explore the badgers' cave; but the tunnel looked slippery and uneven, the walls cracked in places and sagging ominously. They were glad to turn back and escape from the gloom into windy sunlight on the riverside path.

This month the season had changed again, midwinter giving way to January spring, with snowdrops in the orchard, young catkins on the hazels and winter heliotrope sending up tender leaves and scented flowers at the waterside. Blackbirds were trying out their first notes, chaffinches trilling and oystercatchers piping beyond the sandhills. Crossing this stretch of dunes and hillocks, they came on a small van parked under a sandbank, almost hidden by tamarisks and marram grass - the same van, Rowan thought, that she'd seen once on the cliff - and on the sands, besides badger prints, there were human footprints, like those of a man in gumboots, leading in and out of the cave. Sarah peered in from the entrance, sniffing curiously.

"Funny pong. Like nail-varnish?"

"No, it's bananas. Someone leaves them for the badgers, I suppose."

"Do they like bananas specially? Might get some for our friend?"

Uneasy thoughts of the badger-hunters were in both their minds; but the cave seemed as peaceful as before, with no hint of any malign presence. The badgers had clearly passed to and fro undisturbed; the only other tracks were those of the gumboot wearer with his offering: a dozen ripe bananas had been strewn around the gap in the wall where the paw marks disappeared. There seemed only one slight change since their earlier visit: the curious grating over the entrance was hanging an inch or two lower than they remembered, as though someone might have tampered with it.

Meddlesome boys, perhaps? They might reach it by standing on one another's shoulders, trying to get at the row of iron teeth along the foot and drag the thing from its niche in the roof.

A dangerous game. They could bring the contraption crashing down on their heads. Nothing to be done about it, however, only hope it wouldn't happen? But, remembering the lost boys who had played with the sea-mine, Rowan wondered - a word to Mrs. Lilypot perhaps? Then their parents might come to hear about it ...

Next evening, alone in the shop by good luck, she warned herself to take care: to mention the badgers' cave at once would be unwise. She began with their visit to the grotto and the tunnel, and was soon listening to a spate of ancient history. It appeared that the folly, grotto and covered way, known as the Sea Walk, had been built long ago by a rich man home from India, who had also rebuilt Sheepskin House, and made the walled garden, and bought all the land right down to the cliffs. At the end of the Sea Walk, to mark the boundary, he'd set a great heavy door, strong enough to keep out the sea if it came up so far at the spring tides. The Nabob's Door, it was called - Nabob was a sort of nickname he'd been known by - and he'd left orders that there was never to be any lock or bolt on it, so anyone cut off by the tide could escape that way. And yes, so far as she'd heard, it was still there ...

"And - does it open out of the cliff somewhere?"

This careful query produced a moment's check, but Mrs. Lilypot's love of narrative led her on. The door opened into a cave, so her husband said, where smugglers used to store their goods. But the king's men found them out, and there were raids and fights, and a man was killed. So then the Nabob's son, or his grandson it might have been, had iron bars put up over the front of the cave to keep everyone out: the Captain's Gate, that was called, because he was in the Navy. Only later people said he'd no right to do that, down on the shore, and the gate was hauled up into the roof - for she'd heard it was a kind of shutter, that could be raised or lowered at need. And they'd used it again since - in the first war, to keep spies from hiding in the cave, flashing signals out to sea. And in the last war too, when those evacuees from London ... oh, disgraceful, what *they'd* got up to in there ...

For some time, as she listened, Rowan's eye had been caught by something odd. Behind the counter there was a closed door, showing a thin line of light from the family sitting-room; but this light kept disappearing, then reappearing for a few seconds, only to vanish again; as though someone were standing, or rather fidgeting about, on the other side. Suddenly, at this point in the story, the latch clattered and the door jerked open. Mrs. Lilypot broke off to exclaim,

"Father! What is it?"

Old Mr. Lilypot moved from the doorway, shuffling slippered feet on the floorboards. Shaggy white hair hanging in wisps, filmy blue eyes fixed on his daughter-in-law, he stammered some appeal that made her click her tongue and turn to lead him back, excusing herself to Rowan as she did so. Rowan, picking up her bag to leave, looked back to say goodnight; and she had another surprise. She thought the old fellow sent a glance in her direction that showed no hint of dotage. A look ice-sharp, shrewd and alert, while he gripped Mrs. Lilypot by the arm as though he were whisking her firmly out of harm's way.

44

On the next Sunday Rowan was wakened at dawn by bird cries on the steps outside, as starlings and jackdaws cleared the scraps left there for the badger. The night must have been too cold and stormy for him to venture out.

The calm weather had ended in another great gale, beating in from the Atlantic, dimming the windows with salty blasts and flurries, bringing flood tides and the reek of tangled seaweed thrown in dark sodden banks against the cliffs and sandhills. Late that evening Dick Monk knocked at the door with a peremptory offer to Rowan; more like a summons, she felt, than an invitation.

"Asking about the Sea Walk, weren't you? Going in there now - something that needs seeing to - if you'd like to come along?" He was in oilskins, and she pulled on a thick jersey and windcheater, rather puzzled at the lateness of this errand, but gratified at being included.

The trees in the wilderness raved and tossed under racing cloud, and the folly was like a cave of the winds, with icy circling draughts that pierced her thick garments. A gleam of moonlight filled the window spaces, and shone through the archway into the grotto, where the marble Neptune's smile looked menacing tonight. The place echoed with a booming sound, reverberating like thunder, and she realised she was hearing more than the howl of the gale. Dick shouted in her ear, "Big tide coming," and led her through the far arch into the tunnel. He signed to her to go ahead, and walked at her elbow, shining his torch for her to pick her way over the rough paving. All round them the whole structure shook and creaked alarmingly under the huge force of the wind and the sea ahead; but, whatever repair work he might have in mind, Dick pressed on without pause into the mounting roar, as though intent on reaching the far end as fast as possible. She recalled Mrs. Lilypot's talk of a great door, strong enough to keep out the sea, and wondered what might happen if the door gave way. She looked round to ask, "How far does the tide come?" but got no answer. In the pallid gleam his face looked set and harsh like the face of a stranger, not fatherly old Dick Monk. He shook her arm, urging her on, at times almost running, until the boom of the sea sounded so near that she expected at any moment to feel chill foam rushing over her feet.

For some time, behind the crash and retreat of waves and the shuddering echoes in the tunnel, she'd been aware of other sounds ahead; a hammering and knocking, and muffled shouts, as though other people were at work there already. Now, as they hurried on, the sounds became more distinct, and took on a different tone. It came to her with a fearful shock that the knocking was like a distress signal: and then that it *was* a distress signal: and the shouts a frantic appeal for help, rising to screams like the wailing of gulls. She stared back at Dick, knowing he too must have heard and understood. But, instead of dashing to the rescue ... he slowed to a walk, then stood still, releasing her arm. He was smiling.

She took another step forward, and he grasped her again with a shout of warning - "Watch out!" - and shone the light downwards. She saw that they were standing at the top of a long flight of steps. Down there the shrieks and the hammering went on, close at hand now; and she turned cold with dread of something she couldn't begin to understand or credit. The torchlight beamed steadily on a barrier at the foot of the stair: a massive door. Beyond it they heard the surging of deep water, the imploring voice, the sound of bare fists beating on wood.

She broke away, slithering down to the door, groping for a handle, a key ... and at the same time she remembered - 'there was never to be any lock or bolt on it.' She found something under her fingers - a latch, yes! - and pressed it again and again, then shook and rattled it desperately. Nothing happened. The door held fast. She turned with a sob of terror, and found Dick at her side. He handed her the torch, produced a tool of some kind and set to work on the doorpost. While the voice out there continued to howl and pray, she saw that he was deftly removing, one after another, a set of long nails that held the door shut: the door that was never to be shut.

It moved inward at last, then slammed further back with a scream of wet wood on wet stone. As the sea poured in, something fell and collapsed at their feet; an object like a bundle of soaked rags. It crawled up to safety and lay gabbling to itself. She caught a hoarse plaint, croaked out over and over -"locked me in ... buggers locked me in ..." Too shaken to move or speak, she became aware of shadowy figures stealing out of the tunnel, and it seemed to her that they were men she'd seen before, a fisherman from Farmouth, a bus driver admired by Sarah, bell-ringers at the back of the church on Christmas Day, Dick's brother with his grizzled head and eye patch. They gathered on the steps, lifted the bundle shoulder high like a corpse and bore it away.

"They've found one badger," Jamie reported. "Bagged up in a truck near the cove."

He and Pip Saunders had met Rowan in the folly and hurried her indoors, the Monk brothers sliding off into the dark without a word. But she seemed at first too numb with cold to talk. Now it was Sarah who exclaimed, "Is it all right?"

"Suppose so. They'll get a vet to see."

Sarah cried, "But what *happened*? Rowan -?"

Jamie answered for her, "The story so far ... There's a sett in the cliffs, opens into a cave. These swine leave bananas in there, so the badgers won't scent them -"

"*Oh!*"

"What? - well, someone went into the cave at low tide, on his own this time, with nets and a pincer tongs they use ... but as soon as he got in there - clang! - a nasty shock, kids had been mucking about with the old gate, and the gale must have shaken it loose, and down it came, and stuck fast, so he couldn't get out by the beach. No badgers either, the sett had been blocked in, fancy. He had to give up and make for the Sea Walk, only the door had swelled up and jammed ... or something ... and it wouldn't budge. So there he was, rat in trap, waiting for the tide. Nearly drowned rat too, only - what luck - some lads happened to stroll along the Walk, and heard him singing ... and Rowan's going to add a bit of colour?"

Rowan whispered - "Jamie - Pip - *what have they done with him*?" Haunted by what she had seen, she half feared some dark sequel, a deed from *How Green Was My Valley.*

"Cottage hospital, of course. He's not in the best of health."

"No ... Are we sending it out?"

"Ah. Well. You see ... there might be another story. Nothing to do with badgers. Innocent stranger, here for a breath of sea air ... out for a walk ... smugglers' cave, Captain's Gate, Nabob's Door ... caught by the tide, last-minute rescue, snapped afterwards by Nick the Flash ... I think we'll have to make do with that. Just for now."

In the night, waking for a moment from exhausted sleep, she found herself thinking with a shudder - thank God, that's one inquest I shan't have to do.

45

After the clement days of January, suddenly it was deep midwinter. The wind turned north-east, bringing dark clouds that fell as snow inland. Here on the coast there were flurries of hail, night frosts and a biting chill that shrivelled the early snowdrops and daffodil spears, silenced the song-birds and sent them flocking to the orchard to be fed, driven off in turn by ravenous crows and gulls. Wrens and other small birds crowded together at dusk in the dense conifers and thickets of the wilderness, and at dawn Rowan found the night's victims, frail pathetic corpses: a fieldfare weighing no more than a snail-shell, a starved goldcrest like a grey-green moth, Emerald or Merveil du Jour, in her grandmother Minnie's sketch-book, which Mother had found and sent from Ireland.

Oystercatchers, lately so cheerful, now huddled mute by the shore, where a string of race-horses galloped in the grey mornings, brought by their trainer from the snow-bound midlands. The horses were quartered about the district, half a dozen in the old stables of Sheepskin House, hastily refurbished. These lodgers were tended by girls living in a caravan in the stableyard, and a newspaper picture from Far News, showing them at exercise on the sands, brought Rowan a commission from a glossy illustrated weekly: a feature on the girls' daily toil. She spent strenuous hours as a novice learning the routine of a racing stable - mucking out, bedding down, cleaning and grooming and titivating the beautiful restive creatures. Once, briefly but passionately, she had planned to be a stable girl herself, and the work revived her forgotten pang of homesickness for Nine Wells and Grandfather's stables.

Sarah still put out food for the badger; but he was no longer heard, and the birds swooped on it at dawn. She and Rowan told one another that he was simply sheltering at home from the weather. But separately, saying nothing, each lost no time in checking the sett under the ash roots: and found the signs of struggle they had dreaded, smudged footprints, scattered earth and leaves, the scratching-log near the entrance torn up and overturned. Whether or not he had escaped, or been netted and dragged away, he had fought bitterly, and they longed for his safe return. But the frightened captive found in the van had already been released in the cove, too far away perhaps for him to find his way back, if he *were* their friend. And they feared he would hardly want to reoccupy the ravaged sett.

The van, traced to a distant owner, had earlier been reported stolen, but the stranger swore he knew nothing about it. Recovering with all speed, sullenly protesting innocence and uttering vague envenomed threats, he too was released, and seemed unlikely to be seen again.

Dr. Gordon had advised Sarah to stay indoors while the frost lasted, taking what exercise she could about the house, rather than risking a fall on slippery steps or woodland paths. A dreary sentence, Rowan feared; but

Sarah dismissed her sympathy, briskly pointing out - "You come from a family where everyone's out of doors unless they *have* to stay in - yes? Well, in my family it's the other way round, we skulk inside like sensible people unless we have to go out."

The uneasiness of her first weeks had vanished. Now she felt profoundly at home, and even the early darkness held no menace. When not dutifully pacing about, 'ten times round', she spent the days with a small hired radio for company, wrapped in her eiderdown and absorbed in one of her books; greeting Rowan at night with indignant sympathy for girls in the past.

"This wretched Lily Dale, when he jilts her she can't just take a job somewhere else, she's got to stay there for ever, doing needlework and being *reminded* ..."

And then:

"You know, it's tough on Rosamond really, stuck in her home town with all the debts and disgrace - worse than Lily, she *minds* about the old cats ... I know she's being a pig about it, but one rather sees her point."

"She's supposed to show what a noble wife Dorothea is?"

"Oh, Dorothea!" Sarah groaned. "Why can't someone stop her marrying that creepy old bat? A dead loss, in bed or out - Sir James tells them so at the top of his voice, but of course he can't warn *her* -"

"Wouldn't be any good, would it? She's too infatuated ..."

"Yes. Oh yes. Like Natasha. Poor Natasha," she lamented. "That fool Andrei, he gets her wild about him, then says she's got to wait a year - a year! - and goes swanning off - so of course she falls for a man who's *there*, then it's agony, 'why can't I love them both at once?' "

She broke off suddenly. They looked at each other in silence, before she went on slowly, "And ... I sometimes wonder ... if you might be doing a Natasha?"

Peter had gone out of her life for two long weeks; at first hardly leaving Woods Farm, then departing - they heard - to order next season's bulbs in Lincolnshire. But their lives lay too close for this to go on. When he was back they were bound to meet, and did meet, in the shop, at Faro station, crossing Sheepskin garden. At these encounters there was no schoolboy awkwardness, no hurry to escape; only a sober greeting, followed by fraught silence and the same troubled look she remembered from that morning in the orchard house, the look she could never account for. Clearly there were still things to be said, and more than once she felt he was on the point of saying them, then holding back: whether from fear, or anger, or some other strong mysterious feeling, she couldn't tell.

To Sarah, this evening, she admitted sadly,

"I thought I might be. Like Natasha, I mean. But it didn't happen."

154

"I wonder why not ...?"

"So do I."

"You put him off?"

"It wasn't *me*. Something happened, yes. It was - when he heard about New Zealand. About my going to see Lizzie and Rufus -"

"And Ralph?"

Rowan cried, "But it doesn't make sense! He doesn't know them - so why - ?"

"He might have guessed -"

"What?"

"You're in love with Ralph?"

Another silence.

"Aren't you? He's the one?"

Rowan said in panic, "I don't know! I thought I was. I think I am ... I have to go there and find out. But *he* doesn't know that -"

"Which 'he' ?"

"Oh ... both. Either." She couldn't bring herself to say their names.

Sarah murmured, "This one ... Peter ..."

"Yes, well? What about him?"

"He's not stupid. I'd say he's quick - and deep - and proud as the devil. And ... I told you before ... he's afraid you might find out something."

"Really?" This flight of fancy no longer no longer seemed absurd.

"You'll find I'm right."

"I shan't," Rowan said forlornly. "Whatever went wrong ... it's *over*. Only," she brooded, "I do wonder what it had to do with Lizzie?"

Then one morning the wind changed, the sun shone again, and the post brought an urgent letter from New Zealand.

46

The little grey church of St. Juliot was hidden away in a web of narrow lanes like bridleways, leading off the wooded road from Boscastle. Trees enclosed a ring of shaggy churchyard grass, ancient mossy headstones, grey-green ash saplings rooted in drifts of snowdrops and a blaze of celandines.

Here, long ago in another brilliant early spring, young Thomas Hardy had met his Emma, the parson's sister-in-law, and spent enchanted days in her company. Memorials in a dim aisle recorded his work on the church fabric, her dutiful playing for services. A poem enclosed in Lizzie's letter told a different story:

O the opal and the sapphire of that wandering western sea,
And the woman riding high above with bright hair flapping free,
The woman whom I loved so, and who loyally loved me ...

Lizzie wrote that she was doing pen-and-ink decorations, a headpiece and tailpiece, for this poem; but it was many years since she had seen the place. Could Rowan find time to go there and take photographs of the church and of Beeny Cliff? (And here was a little cheque for expenses: and *when* could they expect to see her?)

Given a day off by Jamie, she made enquiries at Faro station, and planned to take her bicycle on the train to Boscastle. But Sarah had arranged things differently. The night before, absorbed in *Madam Bovary*, she met Rowan with - "*Now* she's slipping out of his house at dawn - just when the peasants would be off to work? Then at night they meet in *her* garden ... wouldn't be a secret long, would it, if there'd been a Madame Lilypot around?"

Mrs. Lilypot's husband, it seemed, had a nephew working in the station at Faro. So earlier, in the shop, she'd pressed Sarah to buy one of her home-made pasties "for Rowan to eat in the train." And then, glancing across at Peter Thoransen, who was waiting in the background, she added -

"Driving up there too, I believe - Boscastle? Tomorrow?"

Sarah noted his painful hesitation before he said,

"I'm sending one of the men, yes." And then, with stiff politeness, "There'd be room, if - anyone likes to go with him?"

Swiftly she countered,

"Could he possibly take both of us? Please? I've been cooped up indoors for ages, I'd love it."

And next morning, when they were picked up at the stile, she found that her ruse had been successful: Peter himself was driving.

Surely, spending half a day together, he and Rowan might find a chance to talk?

But, when he left them at the church, she had to admit to total failure so far. The long drive had passed in uneasy silence, despite her own attempts at casual chat. Soon, wincing from the grind of backache that had to be kept hidden, she too fell silent, and the sense of mutual discomfort seemed to grow deeper with every mile. Serves me right, she thought, for trying to be clever.

Peter drove away to deliver a load of snowdrop plants 'in the green' that had filled the air with pungent bittersweet scent all the way from St. Max. The same scent drifted over the sunny churchyard. The spring light too was heartening, and walking a relief. Pacing quietly about, while Rowan set to work with her little camera, Sarah began to feel better. He'll soon be back to fetch us, she told herself. Then we'll go on out to the cliffs. Plenty of time.

Beyond the coast road, green slopes let up to the cliff top, where they sat among rocks and flowering gorse bushes to eat their picnic. Rowan soon left the others and wandered off, thankful for the excuse of Lizzie's photographs, and trying to comfort herself with the thought of those fortunate lovers.

Still in all its chasmal beauty bulks old Beeny to the sky,
And shall she and I not go there once again now March is   nigh,
And the sweet things said in that March say anew there by and by?

Hardy had written that in old age, when he and Emma had been married for a lifetime - so they must have been happy together, as happy as the Brownings? But for her, today, there was no such hope, no prospect of lifelong devotion or even short-lived pleasure; only this queer unexplained estrangement still, and the same sense of failure and heartbreak that she'd felt all those long weeks since Christmas. She looked about at the grandeur of 'old Beeny', the roaring Atlantic below, the gulls floating like white butterflies in a dazzle of blue and silver; and never in her life had she felt such desolation.

Well - she'd put an end to it now; ask him to drive them back at once - and take care never to risk another meeting like this.

But, rejoining the other two, she found the atmosphere quite changed. All constraint forgotten, Peter and Sarah were looking at a road map together, agreeing on a visit to Tintagel, then a homeward drive by way of Bodmin Moor. Impressed, as so often, by Sarah's tact and brio, Rowan sat down to listen and eat her pasty; and, as she looked out to sea, her thoughts took a hopeful turn, racing ahead to her journey and what might lie ahead in New Zealand. The fee for her race-horse story, and Aunt Lizard's 'little cheque,' had now brought all this within reach: her passage was actually booked, the date fixed for her leaving the orchard house. By then

Sarah's baby would be a month old, the two of them safely in London with Caro, and she herself free to escape ...

"So - you're to write about this place? For some paper?"

Peter's sudden question, spoken in calm and natural tones, brought her back with a start. She saw that the map was put away, and Sarah taking a rest, leaning against a sun-warmed rock, her eyes shut. Collecting her wits to answer him with equal calm, she explained her errand; and this time Lizzie's name brought no visible reaction. He simply nodded and asked another civil question. She fielded this successfully, and told him - "She came here once herself, as a matter of fact. When she was at Sheepskin, I suppose."

His response was astounding. He turned to stare at her, his careful self-possession gone, suddenly white and tense as on that fatal morning; jerking out in a low voice - "You *know* -?" and then stopping abruptly.

She wanted to cry out, "Oh, what is it? What's the matter?" But no words came. She made herself look away, giving him time to recover, saying at random as soon as she could speak,

"I know she came to the orchard house some time or other - she painted the view from the window. I wonder - could she have met your parents, do you think?"

As he shook his head, she added - "Perhaps it was earlier - she went away to China in the thirties, 1932 I think ... so who was living there before that?"

Still with that searching look, he countered blankly -

"Why do you ask?"

"Oh, because ... it's all rather mysterious ... I'd really like to find out who's lent it to me, who owns it *now*, I mean?"

He drew a long breath, seemed to make up his mind all of a sudden, and said, "I can tell you that."

"You can!"

"The name is Thoransen. The same as mine."

"But - you told me - your father never owned it?"

"Not my father, no. His first wife."

Taking in this disclosure, she persisted,

"And then - after she died?"

"She didn't die. They were divorced ... but my parents went on living there. She wanted that."

"*She*? - Mrs. Thoransen ..., it still belonged to her?"

"It did. And it still does."

"Then I don't see ... just doesn't make sense - *are you sure*?"

He smiled a little at that, but she thought there was something grim, almost reckless, in his manner; as though, well aware that he'd astonished her, he was waiting for some new revelation to dawn on her.

159

A cloud drifted across the sun, plunging them into deep shade for a few moments before the light returned. In the blinding seconds that followed there darted into her head a notion so wild and strange that she turned giddy, her heart pounding, her hands clutching at tufts of dead grass, as she tried to steady herself. There was something she had to ask, but words eluded her until she faltered at length,

"Peter. Listen – Mrs Thoransen - her first name. It wasn't ... she wasn't ... called Letty? Or ... Lizzie?"

The pause seemed endless before he answered.

"She was called Anna."

And, at the same moment, their talk came to an end. Sarah opened her eyes, sat up and said shakily,

"Please. If no one minds ... I think I'd better get home."

After that they could think of nothing but headlong flight, by the shortest route, and as fast as possible. Piling straw for her to lie down in comfort, the other two exchanged panic-stricken glances, recalling their first drive together. But Sarah tried to reassure them. Nothing of that sort was happening, she insisted. She'd felt rather dizzy and queer for a moment - just the sunlight, probably - and her back ached a bit, but that was all. No, she didn't need the hospital ... and yes, of course she could walk down through the wood ... Safely at home, she declared that all was well again, anyway she'd be fine tomorrow; and Dr. Gordon, called in spite of her protests, said the same, while advising against any more expeditions 'just now'.

So next day, when the drama contest result was at last announced, and Rowan dashed home with the news, they agreed that the Farmouth Players would have to do without their prompter on their great day.

They were not of course among the winners: that came as no surprise. But they had scored a notable triumph. The cast were summoned to London next weekend, when a theatre had been lent for the three victors to perform on Saturday. Sunday, however, was reserved for other entries 'of special merit': including two scenes from "Romeo and Juliet."

Remote from it all, Sarah was content to imagine the frenzy of rejoicing and fresh rehearsing, the rush for theatre seats, train tickets, hotel rooms; and Miss Pichegru's secret heartfelt thanks to St. Jude.

But on Saturday morning she had a fright.

Rowan left early for a stint in the office; but within the hour she was back, breathless from alarm and a hectic bicycle ride, bringing a telegram:

"Must see you. Very important news. Train arrives Faro 7.30 tonight. Caro."

47

"Rowan, quick - ring and stop her!"

But Rowan of course had tried to do this already. There was no reply from Highgate; and at Wimpole Street she was told that Caro wouldn't be in today. So there was no way to stop her. She might even have caught an earlier train?

Sarah whispered, trembling, "I can't let her see me. Not yet. It would ruin everything!" (And she thought in secret panic - I don't even know what I'm going to do. It seemed so simple at first ... but now ...)

Then, rallying swiftly, she told Rowan: "Look, I'll just clear out. And you'll just have to cope on your own - sorry!"

"Yes, but - what shall I say?"

"Tell her I've gone with the Players. That'll make sense." Caro had heard a great deal about "Romeo and Juliet."

"No, no, you mustn't! Dr. Gordon said -"

`"Oh, I shan't really. I'll just lie low somewhere in Faro. That place you stayed in once - won't that do? I expect she'll go back tomorrow, then you can come and tell me -"

Poor Caro, they both thought. Her visit, so long looked forward to, shouldn't have been like this. But it was meant to happen later, when they could show her the baby in triumph and break their own momentous news. Now, with no time for vain regrets, they made haste to get Sarah out of the house. Upstairs, while she packed herself an overnight bag, Rowan glanced about for telltale objects - the book on childbirth, the half-finished cot quilt - and hid them in Sarah's trunk.

Looking anxiously at her friend's small pale face and heavy unfamiliar figure, she urged - "You'll stay indoors, won't you? No prancing off to a movie in the dark - promise?"

In the taxi, speeding towards Faro, they could think at last of Caro's promised news.

That this referred to some plan of Breck's they had both guessed at once. So far as they knew he was still in Cyprus; but lately, on the 'phone, Caro had seemed to hint at coming change, a new posting: leaving them to wonder - America, India, Russia? Somewhere, Rowan feared, where Caro would join him with the baby, and perhaps stay away for years, so that her young aunt would never see her? The same dread, she felt sure, was haunting Sarah. The unborn third, rolling and kicking, had become a lively presence in the house, and she knew that all Sarah's thoughts were concentrated in hope and longing for the day ahead; but she no longer spoke of the future. Rowan's tentative remarks she now dismissed with determined optimism:

"Anyway - it must be good, whatever it is. 'Very important' can't mean anything else."

"Very important" must mean good news ... that artless notion came back to torment Rowan through the long hour that followed Caro's arrival in the orchard house, as she listened to her gentle low-toned matter-of-fact disclosure. What she heard was not only a hideous surprise. It also meant the wreck of Sarah's loving scheme and all her plans.

It began with Caro's saying calmly, as soon as they were indoors:

"Rowan, look. It's just this. Breck wants me to divorce him."

Rowan was speechless.

"Yes, he does. The fact is ... he's not happy with me any more. Well, he hasn't been for ages. So he's ... made other arrangements. Quite good ones I think."

Turning away, moving about the room, staring out into darkness, then wandering again, she talked in brief careful sentences that might have been - had been? - learned by heart; only pausing sometimes as though to listen with disbelief to what she was saying. Her eyes, meeting Rowan's steadily, appealed: Please, don't mind too much. And don't let Sarah either.

"I knew you'd be surprised. I was myself of course. But it makes sense really. And you see ... it's all happened already ..."

Inexorably the facts came to light, answering the questions Rowan couldn't bring herself to ask.

Before Caro herself had been told anything, while she was kept at a distance, the whole change had been devised and carried out. Breck had arranged to resign from his job and take up another in America, laid on for him by his fiancée and her family.

His fiancée? Oh yes. A journalist, American, he'd known her earlier in London, they'd met again in Cyprus. They would marry as soon as he was free.

"Of course I knew it had all gone wrong for us, long before he went away. When you've been married for years you can't help knowing how ... how the other person's feeling. But I couldn't see what to do ... well, there simply wasn't anything, I understand that now. But when he went out there - I hoped it might be a good thing, he'd feel better being away for a bit. And then - in the end - he just stopped writing. Too busy, I thought at first ... And I couldn't go there and find out ..."

Once Rowan broke in - "But - I'd no idea. I ... never dreamed ... *has Sarah?*"

"No, I couldn't talk about it - not possibly. I was so thankful when you came away - and then Sarah - it meant I needn't go on pretending. I did tell one other person, he's kept me sane really ..."

She paused, and regained her dispassionate tone.

"Well, I had to come and let you know what's happening, now I know myself. Oh, and about the house - they say I'm to keep it, that's all being fixed up, so you can come back whenever you like."

"Caro! How long *have* you known all this? Really known, I mean?"

Quite a long time, Rowan began to guess; long enough for grief, shock, protest to give way to this desperate acceptance.

"Oh ... when I had his letter, of course."

So he *had* written at last?

"Yes, he had to, in the end. To say that it *was* the end. No -" she amended - "I knew before that. At Christmas. He did send me a present - I suppose he felt it would be ... too indecent ... not to. A book he'd got in Athens. And he'd written inside, *Best wishes*. Nothing else. That was when - how -"

"Yes." Rowan thought of other books, borrowed last summer from their shelves, with quite different inscriptions.

Before dawn, as the blackbird began to warble in the orchard and the gulls cried from the bay, Caro came downstairs and woke Rowan, saying huskily, "I think I'll be going now."

Whether or not she had slept, the night had restored her. The dreadful secret told, she seemed both relieved and tranquil, determined to take the first train home; eager perhaps to reach the person she'd spoken of, the one who was helping her.

But Rowan, looking back to their happy weeks last summer in that easy-going household, could still hardly begin to take in what she had heard. Yes, there must have been underlying tensions, 'moods,' an irritable word now and then; but all quite transient, surely nothing damaging; certainly giving no premonition of disaster. Breck and Caro had had cause for deep anxiety on one count - but that might have solved itself in time. Caro had lived in hope, and no doubt tried to make Breck do the same. So why should the marriage have foundered so hopelessly? Something seemed to be missing from Caro's story, some clue or fact too private or too hurtful to be told.

And soon, as soon as she was alone again, she must face what this would mean to Sarah.

Still, at the last moment a happier note was struck. Standing out on the steps, breathing the scent of spring grass and spicy conifers, Caro seemed for the first time aware of her surroundings. Behind the water woods the eastern sky was streaked like a peach-blossom tulip with faint green and silver, reflected in gleams and ripples up and down the river. The little donkey Peregrine came trotting to greet them. Last month he had neglected the orchard house, making up to the stable girls in the yard; now

164

he assumed an air of reproach, as though the defection had been theirs. Watching his antics, almost smiling, Caro said slowly,

"No wonder you both like it here. I'd like to come back - may I? - and see it properly." And then - "I'm glad I came."

They walked up the hill in silence, rang for a taxi, waited quietly together. When the car lights were sweeping towards them up the woodland road, Caro said,

"You'll tell Sarah, won't you." And then simply, "Thank you."

Rowan stood back as the car turned and drew up beside them, and Caro moved to get in.

But all at once, with her hand on the door, she swung round again, saying rapidly,

"No! there's something I haven't ... Breck ... wait, you'd better see this ... keep it, read it, both of you -" She groped in her bag, took out an envelope and thrust it into Rowan's hand. A letter, posted in New York. One sheet of airmail paper, covered closely in handwriting that Rowan knew, from those light-hearted endearments in the books at Highgate, presents from Breck to Caro....

"Dear Caro, This is the letter I can't make myself write. I've tried so many times. Now I must get it written.

Dear Caro, As you see, I'm in New York. I'm not coming back.

Dear Caro, I have to write this somehow. You remember when we first thought we'd like to have a child and it wasn't happening - one night you told me you'd been for a secret check-up and they said you were quite OK, no reason why not, just keep trying etc. Well I'd had a check-up too. With a different verdict. A shocker in fact. You were chatting away, so relieved and happy, thinking I would be too - I couldn't bear to say anything. I kept putting it off and telling myself it couldn't be true, they'd made a mistake. I'd get another test, then another. And I did. But it was always the same. 'A low count'.

To put it shortly: it's very unlikely I'll ever have a child.

Dear Caro, Well. Now you know. I went on putting off telling you. And I wouldn't let anyone else. I kept praying for a miracle I suppose. It got worse and worse, with you always hoping and being let down. And my knowing *that*.

This last year I didn't think I could take any more. When the Cyprus job came up I hoped I'd get killed. I thought that would be best for us.

Dear Caro, Only one way out, isn't there? That's for you to marry someone luckier. You'll be hearing from Perriman, I've sent him all we need for the divorce.

Dear Caro, Please please believe me. I really mean it. Don't make it harder for us all. To show you that's true - yes, there's someone else now ...

165

Mallory has two children from her first marriage. So, as we Americans put it, I'll get to be a sort of father after all.

Dear Caro, No more I can say, is there. Only sorry sorry sorry sorry sorry" - and so on to the end of the page.

48

Back in the house, crouching by the fire, Rowan read the letter over and over; at first in snatches, skipping from one paragraph to another, then starting to re-read slowly; turning at length to the postmark on the envelope.

The letter had reached London weeks ago. By now the divorce must be under way: hence, no doubt, Caro's resolve to come and break her 'very important news.'

So now - what was to become of Sarah and her child?

Caro's future, her new situation - whatever that might hold - was already remote from the past. Sarah's plan had been fatally mistimed. She was going to be left, in that dire phrase, holding the baby.

Bemused as she felt from a wakeful night, Caro's revelations, and now Breck's letter - one thing seemed certain: until it was born, the whole story must be kept from Sarah. This was no time to pass on shattering news.

And yet ... Caro knew that Sarah's immediate impulse would be to reach her sister, to rush home and hear it all at first hand. She would never have let herself be kept at a distance. And *silence* would be unthinkable. Tomorrow - when Sarah was supposed to be back - that must somehow be dealt with.

I'll have to lie to them both, she saw. Invent some tale or other, heaven knows what. She lay back and shut her eyes to think ... and woke in a fright hours later when Dick arrived to see to his Sunday jobs. Sarah would be expecting her. What to tell her? She'd have to work out something, fast, in the bus to Faro.

But at the lodging house fresh news awaited her. Mrs. Harding was gone to hospital, the landlady announced. She'd felt poorly in the night, and rung her doctor mid-morning, and he'd come and driven her off to Sheepskin House.

Oh dear, the woman added complacently - with evident relief at getting shot of her guest in good time - Rowan mustn't be upset. Mrs. Harding was nearly due, wasn't she? And taking it wonderfully sensible, poor little thing ... and would Rowan like to ring the hospital, she was quite welcome? But Rowan could only shake her head and escape, taking refuge in the office, searching out the telephone number, waiting in terror for someone to answer.

At last a brisk voice rapped out, "Yes? Who? Oh ..." Then, after further tormenting delay, another voice said casually,

"Is that you, Rowan? Caro here."

"S - Caro! What's happening? Is it - are you - ?"

"In child-bed, you mean? Well, not this minute."

Feeling ready to faint, Rowan croaked,

"That woman in Faro - she said you'd been 'poorly' -"

"Nothing to fuss about. I sort of tripped last night. On that stair by the lav. Fell down a step or two - idiotic -"

"*Oh!*"

"Wait, it's nothing, honestly. Just shook me a bit, and I started getting niggles, and this morning the madam kept hovering and twittering. So I rang Dr. Gordon, and he brought me here, like a perfect angel - only a precaution, he says ... but look, quick - *did she come*? So what's it all about?"

Rowan braced herself to say,

"Oh, terrific. Breck, a new job. New York. He's there already."

"Is he indeed. How sudden. How long for?"

"Not sure, she didn't - listen, can I visit you?"

"Yes do - tonight? At seven? And bring my bag, will you, they might keep me in I suppose."

"Oh ... how are you really? Do tell?"

"A twinge now and then, that's all. They say, if nothing happens, I can come home tomorrow."

49.

After these hectic days the prospect of a long stint at Quarter Sessions seemed almost to promise a respite. But on Monday, waiting for the first case to be called, Rowan's thoughts were still drawn back to Sarah and Caro.

At least she'd managed to stave off one problem, simply leaving an early message at Wimpole Street: "Please tell Mrs. Harding ... her sister's still away, staying with friends, I'll tell her the news as soon as I can." Nor was that untruthful. Sarah did seem to be among friends. Last night's visit had been reassuring. Sarah was in good spirits, still confident she'd be home in the morning. Meanwhile she was sharing a room with a gentle placid woman, Megan, expecting her eighth child; and she'd taken a liking to the day sister ...

Thus preoccupied, Rowan failed for some seconds to recognize the name that was sounding through the court:

"Dermot Athenry Gillespie!"

Coming to herself with a start, she stood up, whispering to her neighbour, a girl from the Faro paper,

"Oh, do this for me, would you? Can't stay -"

"Just drunk driving, is it? Up for sentence?"

The chairman was too far away to catch these words, but he seemed to guess at their drift. He murmured ominously in their direction,

"The press may be thinking, 'Just another drunk driver,' but -" he paused, and the name was repeated:

"Dermot Athenry Gillespie!"

Still no response. Then, as Rowan hesitated, a messenger appeared in the doorway and hurried across the court, handing the clerk a missive that was passed to the Bench, retrieved and read aloud.

Sentence on Dermot Athenry Gillespie would not after all be pronounced. He had died that morning.

A moment's hush; then the chairman said quietly, "Summoned to a higher court," and went on to the next business.

50

At lunch-time, getting through to Sheepskin House, Rowan found that Sarah was still there.

"Doc thinks I'd better rest a bit longer, he'll see me again tonight. And you'll visit, won't you?"

"You bet I will. Nothing happening, then?"

"Don't *think* so." She sounded slightly dubious; or just bored, Rowan wondered?

Hurrying back to court, she passed a group of barristers in a corridor. To her surprise, one of them looked round, stared and called after her,

"Rowan? Rowan! - please, wait a moment!"

As he came up, she remembered him. One of Sarah's men, last summer. Kim something. Yes. Kim Spring.

At her side he spoke urgently, dropping his voice.

"I wanted to see you ... came here to find you ... *when can we meet*?"

He's looking for Sarah, she realised; and shook her head - "Oh, I'm not sure –" but he persisted,

"I'm at the White Hart, that's not far. Could you come there after six? Please try." And again, tearing himself away -

"I must talk to you. *Please*."

The hotel lounge looked shadowy and deserted; but Kim appeared at once, drawing her to a lighted table strewn with papers. Impatient to be gone, she asked abruptly,

"How did you know I'm in Faro?"

"Oh ... this ..." He threw the papers about and produced a page torn from *Picture Weekly*; her race-horse feature article, showing girls and horses in Sheepskin stables and on the sands, with her own face inset above her name. Turning to confront her, he too spoke abruptly, daring her to refuse:

"It's Sarah. You can tell me where she is?"

This was what she'd expected. And, remembering him from past encounters - a child of fortune, high-handed, self-assured - she had been ready to put him off with one of those half-truths that couldn't be helped at the moment. But he seemed changed somehow: older, more serious. It wouldn't be so easy. She countered -

"Why not write to her? Caro would send it on?"

"I *have* written. Of course. She doesn't answer." He looked at her suspiciously, and went on in a different tone, subdued and almost pleading -

"You see - we didn't split up or anything, but - in the autumn I was going off on circuit, and we agreed ... perhaps we wouldn't meet for a while.

She said - she'd be away too, not feeling very fit, wanted time to herself, but - we'd get together again, later on. We *agreed* that!"

As she said nothing, he pursued on a fretful note -

"Well. It's been 'later' for quite a while now. And I can't get a word from her. So what's wrong?"

"I suppose ... it's too soon? She'll be in touch when she's ready?"

"Why not now? She - she's not ill, is she? Nothing like that?"

"No, no - she isn't -"

"Then - there's someone else?"

"I don't think - no, I'm sure -"

"Never mind. I just want to know where she is. You know, don't you? *Don't you*?"

"Yes, but ... I can't tell you. Not unless she -" Her halting attempts died at the wretched look on his face. Speaking at random, as though his real thoughts were elsewhere, he explained -

"When I saw your name on that thing ... I got myself sent down here, I had to see you. But now - there's something else." He hesitated, then went on rapidly,

"This afternoon - after I'd met you - I couldn't wait, I went looking for you as soon as I was free. A man in the press room said you were still in court. So - I asked if he knew where you live. In case - sorry - in case you didn't turn up here. And he told me Sheepskin, and then ... we were talking, and -"

He came to a dead stop. Their eyes met for a moment, and looked away in mutual panic.

"He said ... something about ... a girl staying with you. *Your pregnant friend*, he said."

This time, as they stared at each other, she felt her cheeks burn, her eyes widen. Colour blazed in his face. He whispered,

"It's *her* then? Sarah? *Sarah* ..."

"She didn't - doesn't - want anyone to know."

"Oh Christ! Why not?"

Because she's having it for Caro. Until yesterday she might have been able to say that: now it was impossible. But she recalled what someone had told Sarah, in no uncertain terms, about prospective fatherhood.

"Because she was sure - whoever *he* was - he wouldn't *want* to know".

He shook his head, bewilderment added to shock and distress.

"I must see her. When? Tonight? *Now*?"

"Oh but you can't! She's away tonight ..."

"Away where? Don't, don't lie to me!"

"I'm not. She - her doctor took her to hospital -"

He cried out, "You mean ... is it born?"

"Not yet. They thought it might be starting - but it didn't." Shaken by the fear in his eyes, she said quickly,

"I'm going to visit her now. I'll let you know."

"To hell with that." His first assurance back in full force, he announced,

"I'll take you there. I'll visit too. Come on - my car's outside."

"Kim - no, wait! You can't ... she mustn't be upset -"

He said gently,

"Don't worry. I shan't upset her. I won't even try to see her ... if you think ... But I'm coming anyway."

He took her arm.

"You see - I'm dead sure of one thing. If Sarah's having a baby - I'm the father."

51

It was nearly dark when they reached Sheepskin House. Brilliant Orion sprawled across the west, and a late thrush pealed from the wilderness. As they swerved over the gravel and drew up, Rowan broke their silence to explain -

"She's called Caro Harding. Her husband's abroad. Supposed to be, that's why they let me visit."

"Oh yes? Well, he's back now."

A lamp shone above the doorway. No one answered their ring. The hall was deserted, no other visitor in sight. Lights blazed on the landing above. Up there, something might be happening to Sarah?

A great deal had in fact happened since Rowan's lunch-time call. Her room-mate Megan had begun labour in earnest, and soon, as though in sympathy, Sarah felt her vague cramps start up again. Now, instead of dying away, they grew stronger and more frequent. She set herself to follow the directions learned by heart from the book on childbirth, to relax and go along with what was happening; rewarded by praise and encouragement from sister, who arrived now and then to look at them both. The doctor who had written the book declared that these sensations were simply 'contractions', not pains. At some point in the long afternoon Sarah decided to write later and enlighten him; but soon she was too involved to care what they were called. Sunset glowed in the windows, and sister was there again, exclaiming, "My word, we're getting on, aren't we?" and sending for cups of tea; but Sarah was too engrossed to take more than a teaspoonful. Now came a pause, a change, a new impulse, and she thought she must have reached what the book called the second stage. Megan was wheeled away, and then sister was back again, telling her -

"You go ahead, dear, not long now, well done -" adding brightly, "See you in the morning then!"

In the morning? The words rang like an alarm, giving her strength to gasp,

"You're not *going*?"

Sister laughed, "Off duty, dear!"

"Oh - can't you stay? Do -"

"You're all right, doing fine, bye bye now." She whisked out of sight.

Her place was taken by another uniformed figure, who gave her a brief scrutiny, then disappeared in turn. In each short lull between her new efforts she realised that she was still alone, while sister's blithe 'not long now' seemed confirmed by such strong exertions that she began to fear the baby might be born before anyone came again. Surely someone should be there to look after them? She tried to call for help, but her labours left her too short of breath to make herself heard. And now terror for the safety of the plunging struggling infant invaded her as she waited for the next onset. And somehow her fear seemed to check the process; the pains came more feebly and at longer intervals. A sense of frustration, of *something wrong* was added to her fright. She lay helpless, still trying to call out, but her cries were too weak and breathless to carry far.

After a long time the nurse was there again, saying sharply,

"All right, no need for *you* to make a fuss, I've got my hands full!"

"Do ... stay ... won't you?"

"I'm on my own, you'll have to wait your turn ..."

"Someone else - then? The baby – Doctor Gordon - "

Rowan hurried up the stairs with Kim beside her; then they paused, hearing voices. The door of Sarah's room was ajar, and they caught a strange hoarse whisper repeating -

"Please ring him -"

A brusque retort: "Nonsense. You don't need a doctor." And the faint plea again:

"He said he'd come. The baby - please - ring Dr. Gordon -"

"That's enough." Footsteps crossed towards the door, and the whisper became a cry -

"I can't have her by myself! She - she might -"

Then, as Kim and Rowan sprang forward, there came a remark such as they'd never dreamed of hearing from a professional nurse:

"Well, you should have had it in the daytime, when the staff were here!"

The speaker bounded out, almost colliding with them, and stopped short, saying furiously,

"What are you doing here? No visitors tonight!"

A bell sounded from another room along the landing, and she rushed away, shouting back at them -

"Will you go at once!"

Ignoring this, they reached Sarah's bedside together.

She lay still, her eyes shut, dry lips moving soundlessly. She seemed not to hear when they spoke. Rowan turned back to make for the telephone outside; and just as she did so, it began to ring.

Sarah opened her eyes, looking up at them calmly, trying to smile as she whispered -

"All right. That's him."

The nurse could be heard answering the ring, saying in quite different tones,

"Oh yes, doctor, she is. Quite soon now. Of course, doctor."

177

She stamped in, snapping,

"That was Dr. Gordon. He said to tell you he's coming."

Brushing past the intruders, she grasped the handrail and steered Sarah's bed away to a delivery room.

52

"I got through to him, you see," Sarah told them. "When she said - what you heard - I knew it was up to me. I called him and called, I *made* him hear me. When the 'phone rang, I knew I'd done it."

And perhaps she had, Rowan thought. Perhaps, at such a fateful time, one might have strange powers. Certainly, at that very moment, Dr. Gordon *had* thought of her, had rung to ask if she were showing any signs ... and then dashed to their rescue.

Paddy, nearly a day old, stirred in Sarah's arms, making small mewing sounds; eyes tightly shut, fingers waving and clutching at her blanket, dark hair lying in silken rings on the fragile skull.

Kim burst out -

"But what did that bitch think she was up to? Leaving you alone? You might both have died -"

"Megan says they're supposed to send to the cottage hospital if they need help. But -"

Rowan broke in -

"Oh, Megan! What did she -?"

"Ten-pound boy. Poor dear, it took ages."

"Well, and where was *her* doctor?" Kim demanded. "Why didn't he come and help her?"

"No one asked him. Won't admit they can't cope, they might lose face, or promotion -"

"Or *lives*! And what about the fathers?" Kim asked savagely. " 'No visitors,' what a nerve - *we* should be there all the time, then there couldn't be a toss-up like that!"

Paddy opened her eyes, gazed about and seemed to fix him with a fascinated stare. He fell silent, watching his daughter in equal fascination; and not, the other two noted, with anything like aversion.

When Rowan left them he came out of his trance to say heavily,

"Why didn't you tell me? Why all the secrecy?"

"Kim. I did ask you ...

"*What*?"

"I said - what would you do if a girl friend got pregnant? And you said - *do you know what you said*?"

He looked at her blankly, too shaken to speak; and then stammered,

"But - God Almighty, Sarah! - Of course I never meant *you*!"

At her look, he amended hastily,

"I mean ... I never meant any of that. You should have known. And what did you plan to do? Not ... not give her up, surely? Get her adopted? You *couldn't* - ?"

"Never," Sarah placidly agreed.

"Didn't feel up to revelations," she explained, alone with Rowan next evening before Kim arrived. "Quick, though," she urged, "What's this about Breck? In New York now, you said?"

Clasping her goddaughter, Rowan hesitated: where to begin?

Sarah lay back, her dark eyes brilliant and watchful.

"Come on. Something's happened, hasn't it?"

Rowan told her.

At the end she sighed,

"So that's it. I did wonder ... And - what have you said to her - about me?"

"Just - you're still away. I've been waiting ... I'll ring her now if you like. So - what *shall* I say?"

"Never mind, I'll do it." Leaning over to take the baby, Sarah added,

"Kim's got to be back in London tomorrow. Coming again on Saturday. I think he might bring Caro with him."

"Oh, but - Sarah! You're ... you're going to keep her?"

"Well, of course I am. I've known for ages I'd never hand her over. Anyway," she mused, "I guess Caro's got plans of her own now. Don't you?"

And the next evening:

"Well, I've told her. About Paddy ... and Kim."

"So is she ... was she ... ?"

"Amazed of course. Thrilled for us. She didn't want to say much about Breck - just had I heard, and yes, she'll be all right."

Still thinking of the divorce, looking back as Rowan had done, she recalled:

"I suppose ... I did realise something was wrong. After you left ... it all got rather frightening. Caro'd stopped talking about him. And I knew he'd stopped writing. I couldn't ask - I tried, she wouldn't let me."

"No, she said so."

"Only ... then she began to change. She stopped looking ... desperate. She seemed to be coping. Out a lot in the evenings ..."

"Yes, you said ... that man she works for? Howard Marchant?"

Their eyes met, and Rowan murmured,

"Not married ... is he?"

"Wife killed in the war. Guards Chapel bomb. He was in Normandy."

Presently Sarah went on,

"So, when I came away - I knew she'd be glad to be on her own. But I still thought it was just a bad patch, they'd be all right again when Breck came home. And then they'd have the baby! So pleased with myself I was. What an idiot!"

181

"Still, you -"

"Oh yes, I meant well. And I honestly meant to do it, till I started having doubts."

"When did you realise - it wasn't on?"

"Pretty soon after that. It got to be a worry, I admit. But I thought perhaps we could share her. And then I told myself - oh, leave it till she's born, it'll sort itself out. And, " she laughed, "It has, hasn't it?"

Rowan ventured,

"It was always Kim, though ... wasn't it? He was the one you wanted?"

"But I never imagined ... never expected ... well, only on the wildest-dream level. He was so fancy-free, I thought."

Till he was afraid he'd lost you, Rowan saw. And, she realised, chance had given Sarah an advantage she needed at the start of such a marriage. Kim's feelings had taken himself by surprise as well as Sarah.

"But I must say," Sarah exclaimed with sudden bitterness, "I never expected *this* either - Breck, I mean. They seemed so *married* - wouldn't you have said? Can't believe he's played Caro such a trick?"

"Wait. There's something you don't know. Nor did Caro, till she got his letter-"

"Oh, a letter, was there? A 'Dear John' - isn't that what they're called?"

"Funny you should say that. Here - she brought it for you to see - read it when you've time."

And on Friday:

"Oh yes. No wonder then. But, "Sarah added drily, "Breck's certainly fallen on his feet. Don't you think?"

"And," Rowan pointed out, "He's not the only one. Is he?"

Sarah and Paddy left hospital to stay with Rowan until they were taken away by Kim and Caro. For several days the house was filled with vigorous infant cries, wiping out the memory of Rowan's dream on her first evening.

53

"We brought nothing into this world," chanted the Dean, parading behind a flag-draped coffin, "and it is certain that we carry nothing out ..."

Rowan waited with Jamie at the back of the crowded Abbey, collecting the names of those present at this stately funeral; to be listed tomorrow in any national papers still following that quaint custom. Her last job with Far News for some time: perhaps for ever?

For the past weeks she had been alone in the orchard house, as on her arrival; but in a different world. Firelight and candle-light had receded to the edge of day. The great sun of March, then the softer April light, dappled the house walls inside and out with glimmering reflections from the water. Woods and seashore rang with bird calls, and fresh springtime scents - willow palm, water mint, wild garlic, bitter fruit blossom, flowering currant, gorse from the cliffs, late narcissi from the fields - mingled with the timeless smells of the river and wild garden.

A sallow-willow tree at the top of the orchard, crippled years ago in a gale, sprawled over a ring of mossy stones, all that remained of the old well that had once supplied the house. Heavy bumble-bees kept their footing on the dusty catkins even on the wildest days, clinging with long sticky feelers; while frail honey-bees from the hives in Sheepskin garden, trying to visit plum or cherry blossom, were flung off again and again into the wind. Brimstone butterflies hovered, ladybirds basked or twirled in sunlight, a pair of chaffinches brought lichen and feathers for their nest in an apple bough, and the hen robin brooded a clutch of milky freckled eggs in the ivy by the steps. Marshy pools in the woods, last month thick with spawn, then wriggling with tadpoles, were now brilliant with kingcups and alive with tiny frogs. And tomorrow before dawn she would have to leave it all.

This evening the wind had dropped. A pale moth fluttered in the moonlit orchard, another of those small ghosts - Early Moth, March Moth, Spring Usher? - that Grandmother Minnie had recorded. Now Minnie's sketch-book lay indoors on the couch, among the last oddments collected for packing; she was taking it out to Lizzie in New Zealand.

On the thorn tree by the bridge the Christmas wreath was long withered, the scarlet ribbons tattered; and the trinkets were almost hidden by knots of young leaves. Leaning over, probing with a finger-tip, she found the little cracker ring she had seen on Christmas Day, and drew it off its twig. Oddly heavy, it felt; and by torchlight, when she rubbed it on her sleeve, it took on a responsive gleam. There seemed to be marks or lettering inside, too black with grime to be readable. An inscription? - but who would inscribe a toy? Not a hallmark surely: that would mean it was really gold or silver? Mildly curious, she thought of cleaning it up, and was slipping it into a pocket when she jumped and gasped, almost dropping both ring and torch. A hoarse protest - "That's not yours!" - had sounded from the far bank, as though a frog had spoken. Her own voice husky and defensive, she croaked back - "Just looking ..."

The reeds shook and parted, and something made its way lightly across the water, hopping and slithering sure-footed from rock to rock: confronting her in the torchlight, it changed from apparition to once-familiar visitant, pert-faced, wide-eyed behind glasses. The imp seen last autumn at the window.

She held out her hand for the ring: "Belongs on the tree."

"I know. I only want - oh, are you Linky? Tabby's friend?"

But she wouldn't be side-tracked. She said sternly,

"We *found* it. In the river." A fingure pointed. "There's a rock with a crack ... fetched up in there. We gave it to the tree."

"Yes, well - there's some writing inside. Isn't there? I just thought I'd have a look - all right? Then I'll put it back."

A fierce look signalled - *You'd better*. But then the child relaxed, shrugged and drew herself up, confiding in lofty amusement,

"My sisters ... they're just babies ... they reckon it's a wish tree. Like a wishing well. So they give it things. You know. Offerings." Backing away, she spun round, jumped for the nearest stepping-stone and vanished into the reeds.

The young moon had gone down behind the wilderness. Turning for home, Rowan heard a stealthy footstep on the bridge, coming nearer, stopping. She asked doubtfully, "Linky?" But another form took shape in the dusk. Catching her breath, she heard a faint gasp like an echo.

Peter Thoransen.

They stood without moving, acutely aware as always of one another's nearness, each gazing tensely at an unseen face. Unseen for weeks, in fact, since the hectic return from Beeny Cliff.

Both had avoided a meeting ever since; but she'd suspected that he often came this way from the garden after dark.

Now she heard him take a breath like a long sigh; and she thought - I might as well speak to him now. Why not? If I don't come back here ... we'll never meet again.

She held out her hand with the ring on her palm, and shone the torch on it, saying with desperate lightness,

"Look. This was in the river. Those children found it."

"What is it?"

"Come and see."

He followed her to the house without a word, and sat watching her in the candlelight. She worked at the ring with a pin and a handkerchief soaked in spirit; worrying at the black detritus until, one after another, the marks became legible.

Not hallmarks; though the ring was certainly gold. An engraving, in tiny lettering. Two linked names, and a date: Erik-Anna. 24 March 1931.

A wedding ring.

She had spoken the first two letters aloud as soon as she made them out. After that, warned first by presentiment, then by his grim look, she kept quiet, her eyes on her task, until it was done and she handed it across to him. He turned it about, glanced at the script, shivered and laid the ring down on the table between them. She whispered,

"It's hers, isn't it? Anna Thoransen's?"

He nodded, asking after a moment, "What will you do with it?"

"I'll give it back. I promised her that I would. *You* don't want to keep it?"

He looked shocked. "I! Of course not. But - are you sure *she'll* want it?"

"They found it," she explained. "I said I'd put it back."

"I don't understand. You said - you promised *her*?"

"Linky, yes."

His face cleared. "Oh, Linky! I thought you meant -"

"Mrs. Thoransen? But I don't know her. Besides ... you said they were divorced? I suppose ... something happened ... and she threw her ring away?"

He stood up and moved slowly to the window, staring down at the river, as he'd done on that evening when he spoke about his parents. The only time, she realised, that we've ever really *talked* to one another. Was this to be the second time - and the last?

Waiting, sensing that this was what he wanted, she picked up Minnie's sketch-book and began to turn the pages, smoothing them absently, parting one or two that had stuck together, straightening the flimsy leaves of tissue-paper that lay over the paintings.

He wandered back, sat down again, and nerved himself to say,

"Something did happen, yes. A crime."

"What?"

"My mother called it that herself. She told me the whole thing."

Averting his eyes, gazing at the cold ashes in the fire-place, he went on slowly,

"It was when my mother was dying. My father had been killed in the Resistance. It killed her too. She got ill. We were alone, there was no one but me to look after her. I was twelve ... It was a bad time. We were so cold ... *Coffee*," he said with sudden anguish, "She longed and longed for a little coffee. There wasn't any. And in England *it wasn't even rationed* ...

Well. She got worse, double pneumonia at the end. At first she'd been - oh, fearfully unhappy, but quite like herself, and she talked all the time about Father, but not - but then later it was dreadful, she was out of her mind, wandering. She thought we were back here in this house. She didn't know me, she thought I was Father, she was talking to him ..."

He paused, and began again with an effort,

"She had things on her mind. Something that happened here. Something terrible, she said."

A longer pause. Rowan began tentatively, "Never mind. If you - you needn't -"

He seemed to come back from a great distance.

"A crime, she'd say sometimes. And then - yes, it was a crime, *but* ... And then again, no, no, it wasn't our fault, we couldn't help ourselves..."

"But -?"

"Wait. It all went back a long way, a long time. She and Father were cousins, she was an orphan, they grew up together on the family farm in Denmark. They'd always meant to marry. But when they were older ... they quarrelled, there was another man, she told Father it was over, she couldn't after all. He came away to England and took Woods Farm. She heard nothing from him for a year. By then - she knew she'd made a mistake, she didn't want anyone else. When she couldn't wait any longer - she came to find him. She came here. Only -"

She ventured at length, "He was married? To Anna?"

"Yes. But - she and Anna made friends, she stayed with them in this house. Anna's house. Anna was expecting a child. And then - and then -"

"*He* found he'd made a mistake?"

"She told me, she kept saying - she'd cry and cry and say over and over --- '*we* belonged together, we always had, we talked the same language. Not just Danish ... she meant ... she knew she was his real wife, Anna never had been. And so ... and so ..."

"Anna saw how it was? She went away?"

A nod.

"With her child?"

He said bleakly,

"She'd lost it. Born too soon. It didn't live."

Yes, a crime.

"But you see," he went on, "It was true what my mother said, they *were* right for one another. We were all happy... till the war. I couldn't imagine their ever living apart. Well, they didn't. Not for long."

"So ... what did you do, when your mother died?"

He shook his head, not answering but following his own thoughts. "That was why I had to come back. I was sure ... if only I could live here again ... I could remember the good times, I could have the past ... and forget the rest. So my uncle came, to teach me, and I still loved the place, the

187

work, but - of course one can't live in the past. I found it wasn't here any more, it was gone. And I thought I didn't want anything else."

He looked at her deliberately.

"And then you came. You changed everything. Only - you're going out there, to your - your aunt?"

"Well - for a visit -"

"You won't come back. Not to me. Can't you see -?"

"No, I can't. We've had this before ... haven't we? Doesn't make sense to me."

"Not yet perhaps. But it will. It will."

Have it your own way, she thought, suddenly tired out, almost wishing him gone. There was her packing to finish ... she stood up, laying the sketch-book on the table, looking about for the tapes that held it together. He was on his feet too, as though for departure, but hesitating. Watching her, he noticed the book for the first time, and moved to her side, looking down at a page of Minnie's work, Smoky Wave, Dark Cream Wave, September Thorn, Sallow Kitten.

"*She* painted these? Your aunt?"

"No, her mother." Relieved at this change of topic, she explained about the moth-collecting. "I suppose she got hooked too, she went on painting them, she even named two daughters after moths. Here at the end, look, the last she did - too busy after that perhaps -"

She showed him the last page, the two namesakes, Rose and Emerald; their names and birth dates printed underneath. But, she realised, it wasn't the last, there was another page behind it, the two corners held together by some fragment, a minute flattened corpse, midge or mite. She teased them apart and found one more painting, one more fragile wraith, soft-winged, blond, brown, fawn ... feathered, dappled, ringed ... and under it: Annulet. 24th March 1910.

The twenty-fourth of March ... Lizzie's birthday ... she'd already seen that date somewhere this evening? Of course: on the ring.

Erik-Anna. Their wedding ring. Lost in the river.

Anna Thoransen. *Annulet.*

He hadn't called her Letty, or Lizzie. He'd called her Anna.

24 March 1931. Her twenty-first birthday. And her wedding day.

The missing clue, the last slot in the puzzle.

And it dawned on her - I knew all along. I simply didn't realise I knew. Details began to crowd her memory, hints and signs, clear as day, from the very first moment ... the tea-things from Nine Wells, the view, Lizzie's picture. And Lesley! - sent here like me. And Bridie, coming to see for herself ...

She raised her eyes slowly, and saw that he knew she knew; and discovered relief in his look, as well as apprehension. He said,

"I tried to tell you. That day on the cliff - I nearly did. But I couldn't risk it after all."

She nodded, too overwhelmed to speak.

Sarah had hit on the truth when she said, he's afraid you'll find out something. Both had been right: Sarah in that uncanny guess or intuition, and Peter in feeling afraid. The thought of Lizzie as young Anna, the victim in that old story, was almost too much to bear.

"Rowan - you see now? She doesn't know I'm here, or she'd never have let you come, in case ... *this* happened. The last thing, the last man she'd want for you. And ... if you go out there ... you'll have to tell her?"

She whispered, "I must go. What else can I do?"

What indeed? Her departure date had been chosen long ago. A year and a day, as the song said: and that, by chance or fate, would fall tomorrow.

And, as he knew - impossible to say nothing of all this. Even if she'd gone there in ignorance, his name would surely have been spoken, Lizzie would have learned of his presence - perhaps, for the first time, of his existence? But now - far worse - she knew in advance what a shock her news must be. Could she bring herself to say - "You remember those two you used to know ...? After you went away, they had a son. I'm in love with him. I shall marry him if he asks me." How heartless, how treacherous ... Not that she'd *try* to interfere, or turn me against him. But that's what he's afraid of. Perhaps I should be afraid too?

He looked at her in silence, reading her torment in her face; waiting for a sign of retreat, of aversion. And now she saw - he's a victim too, as innocent as Lizzie, and far more helpless. Lizzie could escape and make another life. But Peter - once he began to fall in love with me - he must have felt trapped by the past.

Deny thy father and refuse thy name ... That echo slipped through her mind, and was dismissed, as it had been dismissed in Verona. Lovers might escape from their families: but not from family history. They simply had to disregard it. "Peter - that was then. It was *them*. This is *us*."

54

The months of longing hadn't after all been a time of estrangement. Their feelings had kept pace together in silence so that now, without surprise, they found each other at the same point of shock, exhilaration and mutual certainty.

There were endless questions to ask, a thousand things to be said; but they still had all night to say them.

"So, when I came - did you know who I was?"

"Quite soon, yes. Mrs. Lilypot -"

"Well, of course!"

"Someone told her - a ward maid from the hospital. There was a nurse, she'd known your family? She talked ..."

"Bridie, yes. Oh, but - it's all so long ago. Why should anyone be interested?"

"Not long for the ones who remember. Dick Monk ... he used to work for my father. He left when Anna did. Never spoke to us again. Not a word to me, since I 've been back. Never once."

"Yes. I think he and Lizzie were friends, I think they still are. He takes care of the house for *her* - and she wrote and said I'd be coming, and not to tell me anything? Oh!" she recalled, "Those cups and things - from her old home ... he must have looked after them, he brought them back for me ..."

"So - not over for him, is it? Or her either."

"No, no, you don't know her. All these years, she's put it out of her mind, I'm certain ..."

"Not quite. She kept the house? And a picture, you told me?"

"Oh, the picture -I know about that. Ralph - my cousin - she'd hidden it away, he found it when he was a child, and she let him keep it. And the house - she must have loved it, she meant it for Ralph or me, one day? And then 'one day' caught up with us, she gave it to me on my birthday ..."

"Yes. Eighteen, you said. So young. You want to see the world, to see life?"

"Don't you? You're young as well!"

"No, years older. And I've seen life. All I need to see."

Your gloomy Dane, Sarah had called him once ... True. But, she promised herself - I'll change all that if I can – and I *know* I can.

"We'll see the world together. Come with me now!"

At least she had made him smile. "Later perhaps. You must tell *her* first."

Around midnight they thought of food, but vaguely, far too engrossed for hunger; and shared an apple and sandwich she'd kept for her supper, and threw out the scraps, as always, for the lost badger. The night grew chill, and they lit the fire and lay close to it, wrapped in a rug, while her last candle flickered out. She found herself thinking - the farm will always be his life. Shall I really spend mine in one place, like my grandmothers and great-grandmothers ... year after quiet year? Yet already, she knew, there were dreams, hopes, ideas waiting at the back of her mind. (The stables ... empty since the race-horses left - we might breed ponies, raise them on the downs above the flower fields, school them on the sands ... teach our children to help, as Grandfather taught me? And the daffodils, so beautiful in bud: why must the buyer be cheated of that?) Ideas might grow into plans, into a way of life.

We brought nothing into this world ... How untrue that was. Like Ralph, like Peter himself, she had brought a deep-rooted love of country life and everything to do with it. None of them would ever stay away for long.

Ralph ... how calmly she could look back, now, at that long obsession, seeing only illusion, 'myth', as Sarah had done. Because they'd been Lizzie's children there would always be a bond; but tonight he seemed no more to her than any of her family at Nine Wells.

The family ... suddenly it came to her - of course they must have known all the time about the house, about Lizzie's sending me to stay here! *Of course* she'd have asked them first ... No wonder they'd taken it all so placidly.

So, in a way, her bid for grown-up independence had been another illusion; for the past year she'd still been sheltered and supervised, though at one remove. And still an onlooker, through her job, at 'real life' and other people's struggles.

Once, Ralph had told her about a place he'd known as a boy, a greenhouse in a walled garden; a glass bubble of mild air and sunlight, where young peach trees flowered in a deceptive spring, shut away from frost and winter winds. The orchard house, it was called.

Earlier, this discovery would have been unwelcome, even exasperating: a child's reaction. Now all that was outgrown. She and Peter ..

"So quiet. Asleep?"

"Just remembering."

"*Yes*?"

"Oh ... something Ralph said. My cousin ... "

That sounded, she thought, quite casual enough. But he said coolly, on a jealous note, "You know? If I'd been Anna's son ... I'd have been your cousin too."

55

Hours later a sound woke them from light sleep. They stirred and moved apart, sitting up to listen.

The sound came again. Not in the room, but outside on the steps. A soft padding, a faint clicking, like animal claws. Now they heard a snuffle; and the crunch of teeth on an apple core.

She cried in a frantic whisper,

"The badger, the badger - it's him, he's alive, he's back!" And in the same breath, almost sobbing,

"Oh, but I shan't be here to feed him! And the poor cricket, won't it starve, with no one here? Why didn't I think of that?"

He laughed, drawing her down again.

"I'll feed your badger. And the cricket ... it'll find its way out, live in the grass all summer ..."

"Are you sure? How do you know?"

"I've got one too."

"Oh ... Isn't it time - we have to go -?"

"Not yet. Keep still. Keep still."

Then it was time.

He would drive her away, as he'd brought her, from the gate of Sheepskin garden. They made their way down to the river in the dark, releasing each other for a moment to give back the ring, to make a silent wish; then stealing across the bridge and up past the folly, unspeaking, sharing the lover's instinct for secrecy.

The high trees were dense black shapes against a few setting stars; but she knew how each one would look in daylight - young fronds and needle clusters, dim flowers and infant cones, dark pink leaflets on the copper beeches, a yew tree powdered with yellow pollen, new glossy green on the laurels, setting off their waxen candles. The scent of sap and resin brought the old reminder of that greenery shop in Bow Street; and with it came one more revelation. Suddenly she remembered writing to Lizzie, describing the shop and her own homesick response. That letter must have prompted Lizzie to send her to this haunted place.

Clouds hung low in the east, keeping back any hint of daybreak. The birds still slept, the river purred out of earshot, the sea was only a distant murmur. Near at hand the only sound was the flicker of their tread across the grass. For a moment she wondered if she were hearing their footsteps today, or their ghosts walking here together a hundred years on.

---ooo---

Lightning Source UK Ltd.
Milton Keynes UK
04 September 2009

143382UK00001B/268/P